The year is 1861 and the nation is at war. The Western Union Telegraph Company intends to connect East with West as never before, but is beset by enemies. Wires are cut and telegraph poles burned, and then matters take a far darker turn when a repair crew is massacred. The question is, who might be responsible? Could it be embittered Indians, belligerent Confederates, or even the Pony Express, which will surely go out of business as soon as the transcontinental telegraph is completed?

Company boss Ezra Cornell employs a grizzled former Texas Ranger, known only as Kirby, to investigate. Paired up with young company employee Ransom Thatcher, the two men head out across the vast northern plains in search of the deadly marauders. Then it belatedly dawns on Thatcher that if his companion is a Texan, that must also make him a Confederate, and yet another potential enemy!

Western Union

Paul Bedford

A Black Horse Western

ROBERT HALE

© Paul Bedford 2018
First published in Great Britain 2018

ISBN 978-0-7198-2641-2

The Crowood Press
The Stable Block
Crowood Lane
Ramsbury
Marlborough
Wiltshire SN8 2HR

www.bhwesterns.com

Robert Hale is an imprint
of The Crowood Press

The right of Paul Bedford to be identified as
author of this work has been asserted by him
in accordance with the Copyright, Designs and
Patents Act 1988

Typeset by
Derek Doyle & Associates, Shaw Heath
Printed and bound in Great Britain by
CPI Group (UK) Ltd, Croydon, CR0 4YY

CHAPTER ONE

The sun's rays had barely crept over the horizon, but they now illuminated a most unusual scene. The great pall of grey smoke was not what one would have expected to see on a late spring day on the northern plains. Then again, nothing about *that* spring of 1861 could be classed as normal, because after years of heated language and not a little bloodshed, the nation was finally at war with itself!

The roaring fire was stacked high with wooden telegraph poles, ruthlessly hacked down like small trees. The blatant destruction proved that, although nominally on Indian land, the figures enthusiastically cavorting around the blaze were either Indians themselves, or simply did not care about discovery – presumably because their work would be approved of. Under orders from their leader, two of the arsonists coiled up the severed telegraph wire for its removal. Whether it was destined to be a display trophy or for future use elsewhere, one thing was certain, when the next repair crew came looking, they would find

7

serious damage and nothing that could be restored and made good.

Howling in triumph, the men mounted up and rode off, but they didn't go far, because they had much more in mind than mere disruption. The fire would burn itself out, but events were destined to take a far darker turn, and for one very simple reason. This was intended to be a murder raid, because if the individuals tasked with maintaining the line were slaughtered, then pretty soon no one would be prepared to take on such a dangerous job, and the Western Union Telegraph Company would be ruined. Or more importantly, no longer functioning.

Reining in beyond a low rise, the marauders dismounted. One quickly moved back on foot to keep watch, while the rest of the group settled down to check their weapons. They had deliberately struck at dawn, only twenty odd miles from Omaha, but even so it would likely be quite some time before a repair crew arrived. And God help them when they did!

The two heavily laden wagons rattled westward across Nebraska Territory, alone in a seemingly unending sea of grassland. They carried ten men and all the equipment that they would likely require to get the telegraph working again. In the past, the line's many and varied enemies had included strong winds, buffalo, heavy snow and occasionally hostile Indians. Hell, even lightning bolts had taken their toll. But recently, far more sustained damage had been carried out, hence the unusually heavy load on the wagons.

They had been on the move since early morning, when the break had been reported, and it was now late afternoon. Although the warm sun was well past its zenith, it was unrelenting, and the men would gladly have sought shade under the wagons for an hour or so. Unfortunately they had a great deal of work ahead, and an ambitious repair boss by the name of Chet Southall who intended to see it carried out.

Off to their right flowed the Platte River, sparkling temptingly in the bright light. The waterway had long been a lifeline for men and beasts alike, and formed the essential component of the great Platte River Road, followed by countless settlers on their way to California and Oregon. Its sustaining presence explained away the route of the telegraph line, and was also one reason why the planned trans-continental railroad would be taking the same course. The fact that the Western Union men hadn't clapped eyes on anyone that day would have been considered quite remarkable, except for the fact that there was now a war on. Sudden uncertainty about the future had altered a lot of plans, but that sentiment wasn't just confined to the east, as the work gang were about to find out.

The moment that Chet clapped eyes on the large pile of smouldering ashes, he had a bad feeling about the whole business. 'What the hell's occurred here?' he growled uneasily. 'And don't tell me it's buffalo, 'cause them big shaggies don't tote Lucifers around with them . . . or carry off telegraph wire!'

The heavily built bruiser named Vinny, who both

shared the bench seat with him and controlled the mule team, reckoned he had the answer. 'Huh, for my money it's the God-damned Sioux. They like nothing better than a good fire with other folk's stuff. So for all our sakes, let's hope they're back in their village having a celebray.'

Chet didn't answer. He just stared glumly at the wanton destruction. This was far more than casual spite. He knew it would require everything they had brought with them to get the telegraph back in working order. Failing to do so was not an option.

As his wagon finally ground to a halt near the glowing embers, the repair boss clambered down to the ground. Not even his aching back could distract him from the task ahead. Motioning the others to gather around, he addressed them in strangely hushed tones.

'I don't know who did all this, and right now I don't care. We've got a job to do, so let's get it done lickety split. The sooner we finish, the sooner we can get the hell out of here. And I don't want any unnecessary noise, you hear? No hollering, no singing. Just hard work! And keep those firearms close.'

The nine men regarded their boss with unusual solemnity. Normally there would have been ribald banter and laughter, but not this time. All could sense that he was in deadly earnest, and they had eyes. They could see for themselves what had been done. What if those responsible *were* still in the area?

The unspoken question was chillingly answered by a piercing shriek from the south, and quite suddenly the urgent telegraph repairs were completely forgotten. As a large body of horsemen came into view, personal survival was abruptly all that mattered, because there could be no doubt whatsoever that the new arrivals were both belligerent and numerous.

'Sweet Jesus, let's get out of here,' yelled one of the men, a scrawny cuss named Seaton, as he raced for the nearest wagon. There was no hiding the panic in his voice, and such an emotion was contagious.

As the others followed the frightened man, Chet bellowed after them, 'Fort up behind the wagons, you morons, or we're dead for sure.' But no one appeared to be listening.

Boiling mad, and with the sound of pounding hoofs drumming in his ears, he raced after his men. Coming up behind Seaton, just as that individual clambered up onto the bench seat, he grabbed his right arm and heaved him off the wagon. 'Don't be a damn fool,' he snarled. 'We can't outrun them with these. Our only chance is to stick together and fight.' So saying, the repair boss levered a cartridge into the breech of his Spencer repeating carbine, retracted the hammer and fired directly into the skull of one of the lead mules. As that animal collapsed to the ground, still in its traces, as though pole-axed, Chet shifted position and repeated the brutal action with the other wagon team.

'Now, we either all go together or not at all,' he shouted. 'So defend yourselves!'

His startled men, hardened by life on the frontier, got a grip on their nerves and spread out behind the wagons. As their assailants rapidly closed the distance, the Western Union employees levelled their assorted weapons. It was a sad fact that Chet was the only man in possession of a repeating long gun. Of the others, one had a battered Sharps breechloader, whilst the rest were equipped with out-dated muzzle-loading rifles of the type being issued to the opposing armies.

Knowing that he would be needed to provide covering fire whilst his men reloaded, Chet resisted the strong urge to shoot and instead scrutinized their attackers. He had already surmised that he and his men had been lured into a carefully prepared trap, but it was the strange appearance of the charging horsemen that puzzled him.

Superficially, they seemed to be hostile Indians, or at least those in the lead did. But since when did the wild tribes all use saddles?

The Sharps crashed out first, and instantly claimed a victim. Yet even as the painted savage toppled from his mount, the drawing of first blood seemed to act as a signal, because with amazing discipline the phalanx suddenly split into two. Each flank swept off to the side of the wagons at the very moment that the eight defenders opened fire. Taken by surprise, their ragged volley achieved little, bringing only one more man down and wounding another. As a cloud of powder smoke temporarily obscured their positions, the repair crew then made the mistake of attempting to reload their rifles.

'Forget those,' their boss desperately bellowed out. 'Use your belt guns!'

But it was too late. The 'Indians' were in amongst

their vastly outnumbered victims, and the slaughter had begun. The Sharps crashed out once more, before its owner took a tomahawk to the head, the mighty blow cleaving through bone and soft tissue. Chet fired his Spencer up into a looming torso, and was rewarded by the heavy bullet thrusting his victim out of the saddle, but the fight was about to become very one-sided.

Utilizing the far greater size and weight of their animals, the marauders crowded in on the increasingly desperate labourers, disrupting their ability to fight back. The scrawny Seaton managed to scramble under a wagon, but he was only prolonging the inevitable. Although his companions carried a variety of 'cap 'n ball' revolvers, their discipline was poor, and they were overwhelmed by sheer numbers.

Vinny, Chet's burly wagon driver, took an arrow deep in his neck and uttered a high-pitched scream. Another man fired his Colt Navy into the belly of a horse, but the poor beast toppled sideways, bowling him over and crushing his legs. Even as the labourer howled in agony, the creature's enraged rider leapt to his feet and hacked at him with a hand axe. His inescapable demise was grim and bloody.

Instinctively parrying a lance with his carbine, Chet glanced up at his opponent's tanned, brutalized features and flinched with surprise. 'You're no Indian,' he shouted accusingly. The other man merely smiled sardonically and yanked hard on the reins. His animal swung around, so that its haunches smacked solidly into Chet, knocking him clear off his feet. Hitting the ground hard, he lay winded for a moment, unable to move. Peering under the nearest wagon, his eyes locked with those of the terrified Seaton. All around were screams, shouts and the occasional gunshot.

Then, without any warning, the diminutive labourer was dragged 'out from under' by his feet, his fingers frantically clawing at tufts of long grass. Chet never saw what happened next, because at that moment a tremendous stabbing pain of unbelievable intensity penetrated deep into his upper back. Nothing in his life could have prepared him for the unremitting agony. It was as though he had been impaled. As the awful pain threatened to engulf him, he reacted instinctively and attempted to crawl away from it.

Inch by dreadful inch he moved. There was surely no logic to it, because he had nowhere to hide. It was just pure dogged cussedness. And then, as his senses began to fade, his head butted up against something solid. Through eyes that were beginning to glaze over, he dimly made out the bloodied head of one of the mules that he had shot. The last thing that he heard was a harsh laugh, followed by the strangely accented words, 'Looks like this one has met his end. Or is it his ass? Ha ha.'

CHAPTER TWO

Ezra Cornell, a dour individual with a strangely flowing beard, glared around the room at his seated employees. He had been annoyed ever since receiving the message that had necessitated his travelling from Chicago to Omaha. Nearly twenty-four hours spent in various railroad carriages, culminating with the Mississippi and Missouri Railroad line to Council Bluffs, had been a very unwelcome experience. In addition to that, he loathed the primitive frontier life, and especially detested any situation that was likely to cost him money. And this latest crisis had all the hall-marks of being expensive. In fact, one particular acquisition had already set the company back a fair few dollars.

'So how long overdue are they?' he demanded testily.

The manager of the local telegraph office, a habit-ually serious-looking individual by the name of Stephen Ames, frowned nervously. He couldn't see any fair reason why he might be taken to task, and yet the presence of Western Union's chief officer was always enough to unsettle him. 'They should have been back well over two days ago. There were two fully loaded wagons with ten men. Southall, the repair boss, was . . . *is* a good man.'

Cornell regarded his subordinate dubiously. For him, that slip of the tongue had been a clear indication of how Ames really viewed the situation. 'Obviously not quite good enough,' he remarked dryly. 'And the line between here and Salt Lake City is still down?'

The manager nodded. 'But any one of the crew could have tapped into the line this side of the break, to contact me.'

'If they're still alive!' That provocative comment came from the youngest man in the room. Ransom Thatcher, dark haired and broad shouldered, displayed no signs of apprehension. He possessed the unbounded confidence of youth, coupled with the comforting knowledge that his father was high up in the company's hierarchy.

Cornell stared hard at the young man. He didn't particularly like him, but the same thought had also occurred to him. 'Meaning that they were deliberately drawn out there and then killed?'

Thatcher's only response was a bleak smile, but Ames was aghast, because his slip of the tongue had actually been genuine. 'Deliberately murdered? Surely not. Who'd do such a thing?'

Cornell chose to answer that question with one of

his own. 'What other destruction has there been recently?'

'Until about a month ago it was just occasional damage to the poles by buffalo and the winter snows. Since then it's got more serious. Poles intentionally cut down. Wire severed and removed. That's why I sent two fully loaded wagons out.'

'But you didn't think to tell me?'

Ames frowned again. 'I didn't see any need. You pay me to maintain the line, and that's what I've been doing.'

'Until now?'

'This isn't usual,' protested the Omaha man. 'I've never had employees go missing before. It's unsettled the others. No one else wants to take another wagon out.'

Cornell stared at him long and hard, before heaving a great sigh. 'Fair enough,' he accepted heavily. 'So who do we think is responsible?'

Thatcher had no hesitation. 'For my money, it's those God-damn savages.'

'Which ones?'

'Pawnee, Sioux. Who cares? They're all the same to me. They've watched our poles spreading across their land and they don't like it. All I can say is, they're in for a hell of a shock when, and if, Mister Lincoln's railroad heads out across the plains.'

Cornell chewed his bottom lip pensively for a moment before responding. 'There's something else you haven't considered. This country has been at war with itself for just over *one month* now.' He gazed meaningfully at Ames for a moment before continuing. 'What if the Confederacy has it in mind to sabotage the North's link with the West?' He was pleased to see that both men's eyebrows rose in surprise, but he hadn't quite finished. '*And* what about the *glorious* Pony Express? Once we connect Salt Lake City with Carson City, we'll span the whole continent, and those show-offs will be out of business . . . permanently. Kind of makes you think, doesn't it?'

Thatcher and Ames exchanged startled glances. They quite obviously hadn't considered such possibilities, but it was the younger man who recovered first. 'What about the army? Surely it's in the government's interest to provide us with protection.'

Cornell snorted disdainfully. 'You'd think so, wouldn't you?' he scoffed. 'Unfortunately, the great General Winfield Scott has informed me that he has far more pressing problems back east. Many of his regular officers have resigned and joined the Confederacy. Most of the US Army's frontier garrisons are being recalled, and in his last telegraph to me he suggested that we provide our own protection.' He paused for effect, before adding, 'So that is exactly what I have done.'

His two subordinates peered at him curiously, but before either of them could speak, he pushed back his chair and strode over to the door leading to a waiting room. Opening it with a flourish, Cornell called out, 'Mister Kirby, would you join us please?'

Heavy boots sounded on the floorboards, and in walked a most unusual looking individual, even by the standards of the West. Lean, grizzled, and of indeterminate age, he had the appearance of a man born to the harsh extremes of the frontier. A leathery face was topped off by a close-cropped thatch of entirely grey hair. His most noticeable feature was a large, discoloured scar on his neck that indicated some terrible injury in the past. His left hand clutched a Sharps Carbine, whilst a leviathan of a revolver nestled in a holster canted across his belly. On his right hip, a broad-bladed Bowie knife resided in a leather scabbard.

Very aware of the impression that his guest had made on Western Union's two employees, Cornell smiled slightly and waved to the nearest chair. 'Please be seated.'

'Suits me to stand. You've kept me waiting in that room long enough,' came the gruff response.

The telegraph boss recoiled slightly. He wasn't used to such a lack of deference. 'Aha, yes, well you're here now.' Glancing at the others, he remarked, 'Mister Kirby was a sergeant in the Texas Ranger force. He carries with him quite a reputation. I have employed him to investigate our problem.'

Ames regarded the newcomer dubiously. 'What do you know of Indians?'

Kirby's eyes narrowed slightly. 'I know how to kill 'em!'

'And if it's not Indians?'

The other man shrugged. 'Huh, what of it? I've killed near enough anything that walks or crawls.'

It was Thatcher who spoke next. Staring pointedly

19

at the massive Colt Walker, he enquired, 'Does that museum piece actually work?'

'You're likely to find out,' Cornell quickly announced with a completely deadpan expression. 'Because you'll be going with him when you lead the next repair crew out of here.'

The young man opened and closed his mouth in stunned silence, and it was left to Kirby to respond. 'Say what?' he growled ominously.

'You heard me, and it's non-negotiable,' Cornell retorted.

'I don't rightly know what that means, but I only work with people that I know.'

'So get to know him,' Ezra Cornell barked. He was clearly a man well used to getting his own way. 'This young man is supposedly employed by the company as a trouble-shooter, so now is his chance to prove himself. His father tells me that he knows how to use that fancy firearm strapped to his hip, and he can also recognize all the members of the missing repair crew by sight. He also knows the territory, which is more than you do. *And*, since I only know you by repute, I also want a Western Union employee to go with you. I've already agreed to pay you handsomely, and so those are my terms. Take it or leave it!'

The former ranger drew in a deep breath, as he mulled over his very limited options. Finally he hoicked up a gobbet of phlegm, and was on the point of dispatching it to the floor when he suddenly recalled his situation. Grimly swallowing it, he replied, 'I guess I'll take it.' Then, fastening his steely eyes on

20

Ransom Thatcher, he added, 'Just don't get in my way, boy!'

The two men stood outside Western Union's office and regarded each other uneasily: Kirby because the younger man was purely an unwanted encumbrance, and Thatcher because the older man made him both nervous and more than a little curious. It was Thatcher who finally spoke first.

'You never did answer my question about that old Colt.'

His companion, because in truth that's what they now were to each other, carefully scrutinized his unfamiliar surroundings. On the face of it, Omaha had little to boast about. Its existence was all down to its location on the frontier. Situated on the west bank of the Missouri river, it had been founded only seven years earlier by land speculators from neighbouring Council Bluffs, directly across the river in the State of Iowa. Its buildings, some little more than shacks, were mostly constructed of rough-cut timber. In the early days, claim jumping had been rife, and only brought under control by vigilante justice. The stated intention was for the city to be the starting point for the Union Pacific Railroad, as it set off westward across the plains, but that was for the future.

Kirby obviously found what he was looking for because, in one seemingly fluid motion, he drew, cocked and fired his huge revolver. The heavy ball flew unerringly towards a heavy black bell outside a blacksmith's forge. The distance must have been a touch

21

over seventy yards, but it struck dead centre. The tremendous clanging noise caused a burly figure to erupt from the forge, but when he spotted the revolver still pointing in his direction he wisely scooted back in again.

'That man was no fool,' Kirby observed as he holstered the smoking weapon. 'Let's hope any enemies on the plains are as easily despatched.'

Ransom Thatcher was impressed, but he was also young and vain, and he just couldn't resist the temptation to match the shot. Drawing his own, very unusual weapon, he squeezed his middle finger, which had the effect of cocking the handsome looking revolver. He was just on the point of firing when Kirby interrupted.

'What the hell is that piece, anyhu?'

'It's called a Savage.'

'Huh, you'll likely meet some of those where we're headed!'

Thatcher's only answer was to squeeze his forefinger. There was a satisfying crash followed by a rather more muted clang. The second ball had just glanced off the left side of the bell. Nevertheless, it was remarkably good shooting, and this time the blacksmith didn't even bother to put in an appearance.

'If you can do that under fire, you might just come in useful,' the older man allowed. With that, he turned and walked off, calling back over his shoulder, 'Let's go find us some willing workers.'

As it turned out, the workers proved to be extremely

far from willing. Surly and ill tempered, they regarded their new boss with ill-concealed scorn.

'I've heard what happened to the last crew,' sneered a particularly hostile individual named Clayton. Lean and pock-marked, he appeared to be the spokesman.

'You've no more idea what's happened to them than we have,' Thatcher retorted. 'For all you know, they might have been tempted by a cash bounty and joined the Union Army.'

'Yeah, well that might not be a bad idea, the way this job's shaping up.'

Thatcher placed his hands on hips and gazed around at the rest of the men. 'You're all employed by the Western Union to maintain the line, and that's what you're going to do. Any man that won't come with me can draw his pay and leave now.'

Some of the men licked their lips nervously, but none took him up on that. Jobs were not that easy to come by on the frontier. And yet they were obviously very scared. It was left to the belligerent Clayton to speak. 'It's all very well you saying that, but who's going to protect us? Where's those damn bluecoats when we need them?'

'I'll guarantee your miserable hides,' announced the scarred, grim-faced individual, whom none of them had ever seen before.

'And just who the hell are you?'

Kirby chose to answer that question with one of his own. 'Any of you fellas ever heard of John Coffee Hays?'

Clayton's eyes widened considerably. 'The famous Comanche killer from down Texas way?'

Kirby nodded. 'The very same. I was a sergeant in his ranger company, and we *never* backed off from a fight. An' we gave the greasers a good licking in the Mexican War as well. So you just come along with us. Anyone trying to take your scalp will be paroled to Jesus before you can say Santa Anna!'

From behind them, and without any warning, came the loud and authoritative voice of Ezra Cornell. 'Mister Thatcher and his new friend have shown you the stick, and now I will show you the carrot.' The telegraph boss knew that some of the men would probably have little idea of his meaning, but what he said next could not be misunderstood by anyone. 'Every man that goes out with Mister Thatcher will get a bonus of fifty dollars each, in cash ... *when* the telegraph is back in operation. So stop sashaying around, get on those wagons and move out, before I change my mind.'

Fifty dollars was a lot of money to such men. They looked at each other and then at Clayton, and he nodded. As they finally moved off to comply, Cornell edged closer to the young trouble-shooter and murmured, 'But they'll have to be alive to claim the bonus, of course.'

As Thatcher regarded him with open-mouthed shock, he added, 'Just make damn sure that you get the line repaired. Once we span this continent, we'll be able to charge one whole dollar for each and every word sent. Just think of that. One dollar *a word*.

24

Huzzah!' For a moment his eyes seemed to shine with a burning intensity, before he turned on his heels and stalked off.

Kirby had overheard the exchange, and couldn't resist a sardonic smile. 'When it comes right down to it, you city slickers ain't a whole lot different from the rest of us. You just use fancier words, is all!'

CHAPTER THREE

It was late in the day. Darkness would soon fall across the plains, and thus far all they had seen was an uninterrupted line of poles, with the attendant unbroken telegraph line flowing gracefully from one to the other.

'We're gonna have to make camp soon,' Clayton called mournfully from his seat on the lead wagon. 'Else we won't be able to see our way forward.'

Thatcher, some distance off to the left, merely waved his acknowledgement. He was actually in agreement, but somewhat pre-occupied by the strange behaviour of his riding companion. The two men were on horseback, and therefore thankfully free of the foul-smelling labourers. Although, to be fair, he didn't consider Kirby to be any bed of roses either. In fact the further west they went, the worse the stink seemed to get. Then, after weaving from side to side for a while, the former ranger abruptly reined in and sat ramrod straight in his saddle.

'What do you make of that stench, Thatcher?' he demanded.

Taken by surprise, the younger man flinched slightly. To give himself time to respond, he ostentatiously sniffed the air. Somewhat guiltily, he realized that the sickly sweet smell couldn't possibly be emanating from the Texan. 'What on earth can it be?' he finally replied.

By way of answer, Kirby wheeled his mount around, pointed directly at the first wagon and gestured firmly for them to stop. 'Wait here until I say otherwise,' he ordered. Then, drawing his 'horse pistol', he softly remarked to Thatcher, 'Get that fancy shooting iron out and follow me.'

Watching both men ride off with weapons drawn, Clayton exclaimed, 'Aw shit, this suddenly ain't worth no fifty dollars,' and grabbing his old shotgun from under the bench seat, he added, 'Better arm yourselves, boys. Just in case.'

The two horsemen advanced across the undulating grassland, topped a small rise and were soon out of sight of the wagons. The gruesome scene that awaited them immediately pushed any concern for the nervous workmen completely from their minds.

'Looks like we've found the missing repair crew,' Kirby muttered. 'What's left of them.'

And found them they had. Both wagons and all their contents had been burned down to ashes. Only the blackened iron tools and fittings remained. All around lay stiffened and bloodied corpses. Some had been scalped and others brutally hacked at. One body had been casually tossed into the inferno, and was now barely recognizable as a human being. Although the fire had long since burnt out, the embers were still warm, and the awful smell of burnt flesh lingered on the wind.

Thatcher was visibly shaken. 'God-damned savages,' he snarled. 'Why do they have to make such a mess of a man?'

The other's response to that amazed him. 'Weren't any Indians did this.'

'How can you tell that?'

'Because they look too damn good, that's how!' Kirby retorted angrily. Reining in close to the ashes, he dismounted and carefully scrutinized his awful surroundings. Unlike the younger man, he wasn't overwhelmed by emotion, because such sights were not new to him. Gazing silently around, he reconstructed the course of events. Then, realizing where the attack had come from, he clambered back into the saddle and moved off away from the river.

'Check for survivors,' he instructed. 'I'm going to take a look-see.' He knew full well that there wouldn't be any, but it would keep his distraught companion occupied and out of his way for a while.

Ransom Thatcher had never seen anything like it in his life – so much so that he barely noted the other man's departure. It suddenly occurred to him that this was what the war between the states would be like, once they all got around to some proper fighting. Wandering around in a haze, staring at the bloodied bodies, he began to speculate on just what the Texan could possibly have meant about their condition. It was then that he suddenly heard something that raised the hairs on the back of his neck. A vague murmur that was immediately drowned out by the noisy and unexpected arrival of the two wagons.

As the shocked repair gang came to a halt nearby, he impatiently demanded silence, and then listened intently. A short distance away there lay a broad-shouldered individual with a blood-coated lance protruding from his back. Unbelievably, that man uttered a low moan, and shifted position almost imperceptibly. The primitive weapon swayed slightly, but remained embedded.

'Sweet Jesus,' Thatcher cried. 'This man's still breathing. Lend a hand here!'

The others swiftly surrounded him, and Clayton suddenly proclaimed, 'Hot dang, that's Chet Southall. Have a care with the poor cuss. I reckon he's only still alive because that pig sticker stayed in him and stopped him bleeding to death.'

From then on, Clayton proved that although he might have been a 'barrack room lawyer' he also knew a fair bit about doctoring. By the time a mildly surprised Kirby returned, willing volunteers had assisted in extracting the lance, cleansing the livid wound with whiskey, and then tightly bandaging it. Whether Southall now survived would depend on the strength of his constitution, and a lot of luck.

'He should have quite a tale to tell, if'en he makes it through the night,' the Texan remarked laconically.

Clayton bristled slightly at the tone. 'So what's the

plan, *mister*? Or ain't you got one yet?'

Kirby's eyes narrowed, and he walked slowly and deliberately over to the labourer until they were almost nose to nose. 'Oh, I got a plan all right, but first off you an' me need to get something settled. I directed you to stop the wagons, but you just blundered on in here. Whoever done all this could have been waiting on just that occurrence. So from now on, when I tell you to do something, you'll do it, or I'll take this beast of a revolver to the side of your head. Savvy?'

Clayton, although lean, was no lightweight. He balled his fists and glared belligerently at the grey-haired Texan. And yet, as their eyes locked, he was suddenly assailed by uncertainty. There was something about the other man's calm assurance and ice-cold demeanour that rang warning bells. The labourers were all rough and ready, hard men, but this former ranger was something quite different. He had the mark of an assassin.

Mind made up, Clayton drew in a deep, steadying breath and consciously relaxed his hands. Then he offered an almost imperceptible nod of assent, and began to turn away. But Kirby hadn't finished with him yet.

'Say it!' he barked. And then, as the other man's eyes widened in surprise, he delivered a stinging, open-handed slap to his face. 'Say it!'

With unwelcome tears staining his eyes, Clayton swallowed hard and finally responded. 'I savvy.'

A chill smile formed on Kirby's granite features,

and he stepped back a couple of paces. 'Fair enough,' he responded evenly. 'So you want a plan. Well here it is. I reckon whoever did this is long gone. They probably thought they'd done enough damage for a while, and that maybe you'd bring the army with you this time. So tonight we're gonna make a cold camp, just in case I'm wrong, and then tomorrow you fellas will do what you came here for and repair the line. Thatcher and me are going after whoever done all this. If that fella wakes up again, he'll maybe have things to tell us, but I already know it weren't Indians. All their animals had shod hoofs, and although this butcher's yard looks bad to you, it ain't anything like as nasty as they'd have left it. So dime to a dollar, it's white men posing as Sioux, or Cheyenne, or whatever you have this far north. Maybe it's the Confederacy showing its mettle, or just maybe it's someone else with a grudge. An' I ain't talked so much since I laid my pa to rest.'

The work gang received his words with mute acceptance and little surprise. After all, they had ventured out on to the plains to do a job of work, and he hadn't really told them anything that altered that. Not so Ransom Thatcher. A penny had just dropped in his mind with a resounding crash. Suddenly wide-eyed with horrified alarm, his right hand dropped to the butt of his revolver.

'It's just come to me. If you're from Texas that makes you a Southerner,' he blurted out accusingly. 'A *Confederate*!'

Kirby made no move for his own weapon, and

31

merely favoured him with a lopsided grin. 'Yeah, it do, don't it?'

The casual response stunned Thatcher. 'So how in God's name can we trust you? For all we know, you might be in league with the murderers that did this.'

The Texan laughed out loud. 'You need to lighten up some, mister. Your boss knows full well what I am, and what I've been, and he didn't pay no mind. I've had my fill of wars. Don't reckon to get involved with another. I'm probably well over the age limit, anyhu. And when it comes down to it, Cornell's paying me top dollar to do a job, and I aim to see it through. So if you're quite finished, we all need to get situated before it gets full dark.'

Thatcher shook his head in disbelief. He really couldn't think of a good answer. But as the whole group broke up to attend to their various tasks, he silently vowed to keep a very close eye on Mister Kirby, first name unknown.

It was a mostly nervous group of men who, lying under the shelter of the two great wagons, watched the arrival of first light. They had all been awake for some time, weapons at the ready, because Kirby knew only too well that dawn was the most dangerous period of any new day. Many a foe had attacked at such a time, in the hope that their victims would be groggy with sleep and unprepared.

On this occasion however, they remained unmolested, and after a cheerless breakfast of biscuit washed down with river water, the labourers began work replacing the telegraph poles.

Maybe it was the noisy activity, or a desperate need for liquid, but shortly afterwards Chet Southall's eyes abruptly snapped open. Kirby, anxious to be back in the saddle, gave the poor man little time to regain his senses.

'Who was it done this to you?' he demanded, displaying scant sympathy.

Southall flinched, seemingly at the harsh questioning, and it was some time before he was able to gather his thoughts. His eyes searched around for a friendlier face, and found one in the shape of Thatcher's younger, gentler features. Thatcher smiled, and murmured, 'Take your time. You're amongst friends now.'

Kirby huffed and puffed impatiently, but otherwise managed to hold his tongue.

It wasn't long before their patience was rewarded. 'They were white men, with some of them passing themselves off as Indians,' Southall managed. His speech was painfully slow, but he had definitely regained his wits. 'The bastards knew their business. They came out of nowhere and split up just before we fired. We never stood a chance.'

The Texan nodded at the confirmation of his theory, and was about to move away.

'One other thing,' the repair boss croaked. 'One of them spoke with a strange accent.'

Kirby regarded him curiously. 'What kind of accent?'

The wounded man stared at him long and hard before answering. 'He sounded like you!'

REPAIR CREW FOUND – STOP – ONE SUR-
VIVOR – STOP – WHITE MEN RESPONSIBLE –
STOP – KIRBY AND THATCHER IN PURSUIT –
STOP – IF POSSIBLE SEND HELP TO
FREMONT – STOP

'Huh,' grunted Thatcher. 'Knowing Cornell, he'll probably deduct nineteen dollars from my pay for that message.'

The two men had watched as one of the crew had patched into the unbroken connection back to Omaha and tapped out the message on a portable telegraph key. Now it was time to live up to the bold words.

'You right sure you want to catch up with those cockchafers?' the young man queried dubiously. 'We're going to be a mite outnumbered.'

Kirby regarded him speculatively. 'Like I said earlier, I'm being paid to do a job. If you ain't up to it, then maybe you should just return to Omaha with the crew.'

Thatcher's eyes boggled. 'You'd go on alone, even without knowing the area?'

The Texan's response was coated with iron, as he unconsciously touched the scar on his neck. 'I can read sign and follow a trail. This Sharps'll do the rest.'

Thatcher was beginning to understand the calibre of the man he had been assigned to. 'Well, I'm no quitter,' he affirmed. 'So I'll be seeing this through with you.'

34

Kirby nodded and offered the makings of a smile. 'I kind of thought you might.'

Ransom Thatcher took a last look at the repair crew before they disappeared from sight over the rise. Already a good number of new poles had been sunk into the ground. The workmen had been far from happy at losing their escort, but the task was coming on apace, their uncommon speed no doubt motivated by fear. They would definitely be on their way back to Omaha before nightfall.

'What settlements are there around these parts?' Kirby asked, as they jogged along side by side.

'None to speak of, once we get clear of the Platte River. Those that do exist near it, are mainly there anticipating the arrival of the railroad. Fremont's the nearest town to the massacre. That's why I asked for any help to be sent there. But of course, there's no way of us knowing whether Cornell actually sends any. I guess it'll depend on how keen he is to spend some more money. We'll just have to take him on trust.'

Pointedly avoiding his companion's searching glance, the young man paused briefly, as something else occurred to him. 'South of here, the Pony Express will have swing stations every twenty miles or so. They begin in St Joseph, Missouri and stretch northwest up towards the Platte and then follow the river west. There sure ain't any love lost between them and the Western Union.'

Kirby nodded. 'Yeah, well it would make sense for us to visit with one then, wouldn't it? See if they've had any trouble with these desperados, or if they mean us any. Besides, I could sure use some hot coffee.'

Thatcher was puzzled. 'But what about this trail we're following?'

Kirby offered a genuine chuckle. 'Huh, a blind man on a galloping horse could pick this up again. Besides, I've a feeling it could just lead us straight to one of these swing stations. Raiders far from home are gonna need remounts.' With that, he urged his horse to greater speed, as though instinctively sensing that there could be more than just coffee brewing.

CHAPTER FOUR

They heard the gunfire long before there was anything to see. It came in bursts of rapid firing, as though there were a lot of people involved. The two men exchanged meaningful glances before continuing south with renewed speed. Advancing into strong sunlight, they kept their hat brims low, and Kirby was already working on a likely strategy.

The sight that eventually greeted them was a whirl of sound and motion. Leaving their horses ground tethered with army issue picket pins, the Western Union agents had cautiously proceeded up a small rise. Contrary to popular belief, the plains were not just flat and featureless. So it was without any great surprise that they found themselves looking down on a shallow basin of sorts, which afforded a modest amount of shelter from the often relentless wind.

Due to the almost total lack of trees, a large cabin had been constructed out of prairie 'marble', as sod was jokingly referred to. Timber, expensively freighted west by wagon, had been used for the doors, windows and the substantial corral. From the number of horses held in the latter structure, the small settlement was obviously a swing station for the Pony Express. And that fact explained why it was currently under siege from a large band of horsemen. The attackers had obviously attempted to run off the remounts, but had met unexpectedly stiff resistance. Two bodies, blood-ied and still, lay near the corral, and puffs of gunsmoke appeared at the single door and two windows. A horse, saddled and ready to go, was teth-ered to a hitching post just outside of the cabin.

Kirby grunted. 'I reckon one of the relay riders had pulled in just before these buzzards attacked. So they're up against three guns, and that sod is proof against any number of Lucifers.'

Watching the raiders, as they rode to and fro shoot-ing wildly into the primitive structure, Thatcher was plainly unsure what to do next. 'There's an awful lot of them fellas,' he remarked doubtfully. 'How do you reckon we should handle this?'

Kirby snorted with derision. 'Huh, are you asking me? A rebellious Texan, who likely wants to cut your northern heart out?'

'Yes. Yes I am, God damn it,' Thatcher defiantly responded. 'And you can't rightly blame me for my suspicions, all things considered.'

The older man stared hard at him for a moment before speaking. 'I can maybe see how you might feel that way,' he grudgingly remarked. 'So OK, this is what we're gonna do.'

The plan was simple and took little explaining, and

the two men were soon retrieving their animals. Knowing that they were unlikely to be overheard, they galloped around the outside of the basin until they found themselves on the far side . . . with the sun behind them.

'This should give us an edge,' Kirby muttered, as they dismounted and again picketed their horses. 'Is that Henry as fast as they say it is?' he asked, as Thatcher slid the impressively shining weapon from its leather scabbard.

The young man nodded. 'It's a peach of a gun, an' no mistake.'

'Hmm, we'll see,' the Texan retorted, as they scrambled up the slope. 'Spread out a bit. We need them to think they're up against some serious numbers. I'll go for a kill shot with this Sharps first. Then you open up kind of rapid, and aim for the animals. There's nothing takes the starch out of a man like killing his horse when he's in the saddle.'

They reached the crest and lay down about ten feet apart. Below them, in the shallow depression, the raiders appeared to be tightening the circle prior to a sudden rush. They were a decidedly strange mishmash, with some wearing animal furs and leggings, whilst others wore unfamiliar butternut grey tunics and caps that possessed an unquestionably military flavour. Their striking appearance uncomfortably reminded the former ranger of a gang of Comancheros that he had once come up against, many years earlier in Texas. The bunch before them, numbering well in excess of thirty, very likely considered that a successful outcome

39

was a foregone conclusion.

As Thatcher levered in a cartridge from the Henry's cylindrical magazine, Kirby retracted the hammer of his breechloader, and took careful aim. Given such close range, the shot was never in doubt, even with a moving target. The powerful gun crashed out, and a rider jerked with shock, before toppling forward off his horse. Even as he hit the ground, blood from the mortal wound had begun to soak into his jacket.

Kirby had just dropped the falling breechblock to reload when Thatcher opened fire, and to anyone used only to single shot weapons, the display was quite amazing. As the young man worked the under lever with practised speed, bullet after bullet flew at the star- tled horsemen. As the legs of first one animal and then another buckled under their riders, the suddenly beleaguered marauders realized that it was now they who were under attack.

With the corralled remounts abruptly forgotten, the men angrily wheeled about in search of their unknown assailants. They soon realized where the deadly fire was coming from, but with the sun in their eyes they couldn't identify anyone. Inside the cabin, someone realized that help had arrived and let rip with an excited, 'Yeehaa!'

Then the Sharps crashed out again, shattering someone's skull like a ripe melon, and one of the intruders cried out, 'The hell with this!' Yanking on the reins, he frantically urged his horse away from the sod cabin.

As he levered in another metallic cartridge from

40

the dwindling magazine, Thatcher felt the spring-loaded magazine tab pressing against his left hand, and shifted his grip. Exhilaration coursed through his body at the prospect of such a one-sided victory. 'Pour it into them, boys,' he cunningly bellowed out. 'Kill every last one of those sons of bitches!'

Instinctively realizing that they had to maintain the pressure, he fired the Henry until it was empty, then simply discarded it and shifted position. As he drew his Savage, the comforting roar of the Sharps sounded off again, and yet another man died. That big gun might not have the speed, he decided, but it sure as hell possessed heft!

Kirby swiftly slid a paper cartridge into the breech, retracted the under lever and then searched for another victim. One of the raiders, still dazzled by the sun, unknowingly came face on to him. Grunting with satisfaction, Kirby cocked his piece, and lined up his next perfectly judged shot. At such a distance, he was using open sights, and so the man's face swam fully into view. His hard features were now covered with a beard, but even so there could be no doubt.

'Sweet Jesus,' he exclaimed. 'Seward!' With his finger poised on the second of the double triggers, the Texan froze with shock. How long he remained like that, he had no idea, but when some sixth sense made him glance sideways he saw that, in between shots, his companion was peering at him curiously. Although coming to his senses, Kirby nevertheless adjusted his aim before firing. For the first time that day, one of his

41

heavy balls struck a horse, bringing the poor beast to its knees.

The man that he knew as Seward tumbled sideways, rolled once and leapt to his feet. With great good fortune he happened upon a riderless horse, and was soon vaulting back into another saddle. 'Clear out,' he yelled to his cronies. 'We done lost this one . . . but there'll be others.' So saying, he dug his heels in and raced for the far rim of the basin.

With Thatcher's innovative revolver now rapidly spitting lead at them, his companions needed no further urging, and they all followed him 'hell for leather', heading west and giving no thought to any wounded left behind. Their retreat was utterly chaotic, highlighted by the fact that there were riderless animals, and others carrying double. Seeing that the tide had turned, the cabin's three occupants jubilantly raced outside, and sent a few more shots after them for good measure. Up on the rim, their rescuers cautiously got to their feet and regarded the carnage they had wrought.

'I'll get the horses,' Kirby announced. 'You'd better reload those repeaters, just in case.' With that, he turned away and thoughtfully walked down the gentle slope. He had been severely shaken to discover that one of the murderous gang that they were tracking had, like him, been a member of Jack Hays' San Antonio Ranger Company, *and* a Mexican war veteran. It complicated matters, and could bring him into unwanted conflict with the Western Union employee. 'Damn, damn, damn,' he intoned under his breath.

Thatcher soon had the Henry's magazine reloaded, but his 'cap 'n ball' revolver required a far more laborious process, and one that he decided could wait until he had met with the cabin's occupants. Still fired up from the violent encounter, it slipped his mind that they might not necessarily turn out to be overly friendly. With the possibility of wounded, but still dangerous men ahead of him, he advanced carefully down the slope with his rifle ready.

Badly injured horses struggled on the ground, whinnying pitifully, but of the humans only one individual appeared capable of being made prisoner, a testimony to the accuracy of the man with the Sharps. The hapless marauder, lying on the hard ground and groaning continuously, seemingly had a broken right arm, incurred during his fall from a collapsing animal.

'Hot dang, we sure showed them,' cried out one of the cabin's occupants excitedly. 'Or leastways you did.'

As Thatcher got closer to the exuberant fellow, he realized that in reality he was little more than a boy. Slim, dark-haired, and without a trace of facial hair, the youth displayed not the slightest discomfort at the bloodbath around him.

'Is that one of them new Henrys I've heard about?' he enquired breathlessly.

Thatcher's answer was cut short by a series of gunshots, as one of the men carried out mercy killings of the wounded animals. The other one strode up with his right hand outstretched. Tall and broad, with a ruddy complexion, he was obviously keen to introduce himself.

'Name's Bairstow. Chuck Bairstow,' he announced. 'I'm right glad you happened upon us, I truly am. Those sons of bitches had us a mite outnumbered.'

'Ransom Thatcher,' the other responded, accepting the firm grip. 'And we didn't just happen on you. We've been trailing that bunch.'

As Kirby came into view leading the horses, Bairstow's eyes flicked over to encompass the new arrival. 'What are you?' he asked softly. 'Local law, or federal?'

Abruptly recognizing his dilemma, Thatcher decided to 'bite the bullet'. Maintaining his grasp, he replied, 'Neither. We work for the Western Union Telegraph Company. You may have heard of it.'

As a deep frown appeared on his forehead, Bairstow instinctively tried to free his hand, but found himself unable to. With the boy gazing at them in surprise, the two men remained locked in an awkward embrace until the arrival of their respective partners. Kirby immediately guessed the likely reason, but not so the other fellow. Short and squat and holding a still smoking revolver, he regarded them askance.

'What the hell ails you two? You getting hitched, or what? In case you hadn't noticed, we've got a prisoner to beat on!'

Bairstow replied through gritted teeth. 'These two act for Western Union, Ed.'

Before Ed could react, Kirby had his Sharps levelled. 'There's only one ball in this thing, but it'll kill whatever it hits. And that would be a pure shame, because we knew you were Pony Express before we stepped in to save your skins. So let's all take a deep breath and ease off, huh?'

Bairstow stared long and hard at the grizzled Texan, before coming to a decision. 'Coffee?'

'I thought you'd never ask!'

The six individuals uneasily occupied the foul-smelling sod cabin. Warm in winter and cool in summer, such structures were cheap to construct, but didn't have a whole lot else in their favour. Heavy rainfall could bring the roof down, killing the occupants under a pile of mud, and they also attracted all kinds of insects, rats and snakes. Anyone eating indoors was very likely to find insects dropping into their food from the roof.

Such factors were of little relevance to the wounded marauder, however. With his upper arm badly broken, he was desperate for relief, and would probably have sold his soul for a bottle of laudanum. But Ed was having none of it.

'You'd have happily paroled all of us to Jesus, you cockchafer. Whether we give you any doctoring depends on what you tell us. So let's start with who you are and where you're from.'

The suffering, frightened prisoner gazed at him through pain-filled eyes. In his ragged furs and outlandish war paint he looked really rather pathetic.

'We're renegades, is all,' he optimistically declared. 'We wintered in Mexico, and then thought to try our luck up north.'

'And this pitiable disguise,' Ed persisted. 'What's

45

that all about?'

Warming to his theme slightly, their captive shrugged elaborately. 'Seemed like a good idea to blame all our bad deeds on the dirt-worshipping heathens, 'cause they deserve anything that happens to them, don't they?' He paused and then added hopefully, 'Well, don't they?' With that, he fell silent, confident that he had said enough to ensure his survival. Nothing could have prepared him for the sudden agony that tore through his damaged limb, as Kirby whacked the barrel of his Sharps against it.

As his victim howled in pain, the Texan stabbed a grubby finger into his chest. 'I didn't come down with yesterday's rain, mister. You're deliberately picking on the telegraph and mail routes, and that ain't making any of you rich. *And* I've seen those light grey uniforms that some of you are sporting. To me, that makes you Confederate irregulars. So who's in charge, and where are they headed next?' He already had a pretty fair idea of who was in command, but didn't want to admit that to Thatcher.

Even with tears rolling down his cheeks, the prisoner resisted. 'You sound like a Southerner yourself. You shouldn't be treating me this way.'

With the others looking on in wonder, Kirby sighed regretfully, and again swung his carbine barrel. The high-pitched scream made them all grimace, but it did bring some result. 'Seward. The captain's name is Seward, but that's all you're getting. If I tell you any more, and he finds out, he'll kill me for sure. Wherever you send me, whatever it takes, he'll find me

46

and kill me.'

'Doesn't sound as though you're gonna be much more use to us then, does it?' Ed remarked, almost conversationally. Without any warning, he placed the muzzle of his Remington Revolver on the fellow's forehead, and squeezed the trigger. In such an enclosed space, the crash was ear splitting. Emitting a welter of blood and brain matter, the luckless victim fell sideways off his chair without a sound, leaving the four men and one boy in a cloud of acrid smoke and with ringing ears.

'That wasn't very helpful,' Kirby remarked accusingly. 'I could have got more out of him.'

'Like hell you would,' Ed responded belligerently. 'And what was that about you being a Southerner? You might feel the same as him. And Western Union sure ain't got no love for us.'

Thatcher bristled at that. 'It's like to be the other way around. Why would we want to deliberately do you any harm? There'd be no reason for it. After all, you ain't putting *us* out of business.'

There was a stony silence, as each pair of adults stared at the other with suspicion and hostility. Mediation finally came from a totally unexpected quarter.

'After all that shooting and jawing, you fellas must be about ready for some of that hot coffee we promised you,' remarked the youth brightly. 'Then I'll have to mount up and get moving. I've got a mochila full of mail to deliver.'

A smile slowly spread across Thatcher's features, as

he glanced at the eager young Pony Express rider. 'What's your name, son?'

'Bill Cody,' came the reply. 'And I ain't anyone's *son*. My pa was stabbed by a slavery supporter in Kansas and just never recovered. Since then I've had to make my own way in the world.'

'And how old are you?' queried Kirby, curious in spite of the tension in the building.

'Fifteen,' Cody replied. 'And I can ride as well as any full grown man,' he added proudly.

'I don't doubt it,' the Texan remarked. 'I'd already kilt a man by the time I was your age.' He suddenly glared at the pair of swing station operators. 'But I ain't got any interest in killing you fellas. If we meant you harm, we'd have left it up to those raiders, and saved ourselves some powder. As for the Western Union, well I personally don't give a damn about news from California, and I sure ain't toting any picks and shovels. We're just two men hunting a pack of rebels with murder on their mind. Fair enough?'

Bairstow stared hard at his partner, before finally responding. 'Yeah, I guess so. And there's no denying you did save all our lives, and for that I thank you.'

As young Cody handed out mugs of steaming coffee, it was Ed who asked the question that had also been troubling Thatcher. 'So where d'you think those cockchafers are headed now?'

What Kirby said next proved that he more than knew his trade. 'If they were looters, just looking to line their pockets, I reckon they'd figure that their luck had turned sour, and they'd hightail it either west or south. Somewhere with few people and no law. But it appears to me these fellas are under orders. Seems like they're out to wreck the Union's communications. They weren't just after remounts here. They were also out to stop the movement of mail.' He paused and looked at the Pony Express employees. 'Who are your biggest customers?'

Ed had no hesitation. 'With letters charged at five dollars per half ounce, most ordinary folks can't afford us. So it's mainly government and military stuff.'

Kirby simultaneously raised his eyebrows and shrugged his shoulders. 'Kind of proves my point, don't it?'

Bairstow chuckled. 'Agreeing with you is kind of getting to be a habit, but you still haven't said where you think they'll hit next.'

Even as the Texan nodded, a hard set came to his jaw. 'I know, and I ain't going to, because you don't need to know. Wherever it is, it won't be here.'

Bairstow's good humour vanished. 'You mean you don't trust us?'

'I only trust the guy I shave,' Kirby retorted, before moderating his tone slightly. 'This is mighty fine coffee, and I thank you for it, but it's time for us to be on our way. You'll have your hands full burying all these bodies, but at least you're alive to do it.' Glancing at his bewildered companion, he added, 'Come on, *horse killer*, let's make tracks.' And with that, he placed his empty mug on the stove and strode out of the cabin.

The other man had no choice than to follow him, and together they mounted up. They weren't alone in continuing a journey, though: Bill Cody placed his leather pouch of letters over the horn of his saddle and clambered up on to his fresh horse. 'It sure was a pleasure meeting you,' he said with an infectious grin, and then, digging his heels in, he was off at speed heading west.

'Likewise,' Thatcher yelled after him. Then the two manhunters also rode away, heading north, watched by a pair of disgruntled and confused Pony Express employees. With a variety of blood-soaked cadavers to dispose of, they had an unenviable task ahead of them.

'What the hell was all that about?' Thatcher demanded, once they were out of earshot.

Kirby favoured him with a sharp glance, before sighing. 'You see these grey hairs? They mean I'm getting too old for all this shit, and it doesn't get any easier. That young fella is very likely heading into more trouble, because those raiders surely ain't done with the Pony Express yet. Apart from anything else, after meeting up with you, they need more horses. So whether trouble does catch up with young Cody, will all be down to his speed and luck. But either way, there's not a damn thing we can do about it. Our job is to protect the telegraph, and since we've got no way of knowing which swing station those bastards might could strike at next, there's little point in following him. That's just how it is.'

CHAPTER FIVE

Captain Seward viewed the dispirited band of men with mixed feelings. On the one hand he cursed the day that he had been put in charge of them, but on the other he felt raw anger at what had befallen *his* detachment. Few of them had any regular army experience. Most were Kansas pro-slavery 'border ruffians', attracted by the Confederate bounty offered to men prepared to undertake special duties. Seward had had real trouble instilling any kind of discipline into them, and it was only because they were afraid of him that they even followed his instructions at all. Some had been told of his service as a Texas Ranger and Mexican War veteran. Any man who had ridden with John Coffee Hays had to possess grit, but it was only after he had blown someone's foot off with his Colt Walker that they realized he wasn't a man to provoke.

What puzzled the captain was just how he and his men had apparently ridden into a trap that couldn't possibly have existed. They had fully reconnoitred the swing station and its surroundings before attacking it,

51

and yet had still come to grief. He wasn't even sure how many men had attacked his command. One thing, though, was a certainty. The next swing station was going to suffer, and God help those who were working there. His men needed revenge, and they also needed more horses, to replace those just killed or worn out on the long ride north. Seward had been tasked with destroying Western Union's attempt to link east with west, and he wasn't a man who easily accepted failure!

Maybe it was because he was all alone again, but as Bill Cody sped across the open grassland, he was suddenly assailed by a nameless dread. Although not fully grown, the boy had witnessed bloody violence before, but nothing on the scale of what he had just encountered. In the heat of the moment, and in the company of fellow employees, he had laughed it off, but now its effects had returned to haunt him. Visions of blood-soaked, shattered bodies crept insistently into his impressionable young mind. Glancing nervously around, he patted his animal's withers, desperately seeking solace from the presence of another living creature. Then he recalled that the attackers had fled in the very direction that he was travelling, and his mouth was suddenly as dry as sun-baked rawhide.

As he finally drew closer to the next swing station, Cody pondered his frightening dilemma. He needed to change mounts, and welcomed the prospect of brief human contact, but what if the marauders had already struck and were there waiting for him? What would become of his ma if he died, and there was no one to send money to her? Then, quite suddenly, the station was in sight and all his fears became irrelevant. He had signed up to do a job, and nothing could alter that fact.

When the cabin was only a couple of hundred yards away, the young express rider reined in and stared long and hard at the dismal structure. On the face of it, everything seemed normal. The corral was full of remounts, and a fresh horse was tethered to the hitching post, presumably awaiting his arrival. But why was there no one in sight? Where were the operators? What if they had been slaughtered, and the killers were even now in the cabin waiting for the expected rider?

Swallowing painfully, Cody eased his Colt Navy out of its holster and cocked the hammer. Like most mail couriers, he favoured a lighter weapon, but the .36 calibre revolver was still a deadly piece. As he urged his animal slowly forward, his heart seemed to be pounding fit to burst. It seemed to take him an age to reach the corral. One of the horses whinnied, but still there wasn't a human in sight. As beads of sweat trickled down his face, the terrified youth held his Colt at arm's length. He was suddenly terribly aware that his gun hand was shaking uncontrollably, and yet try as he might, he just couldn't seem to stop it.

The cabin door flew open and a laughing figure lurched out. The man was obviously sharing a joke with someone inside, but as he clapped eyes on the figure of Cody his jaw fell open.

'Sweet Jesus, boy,' he exclaimed, taking an involuntary step back. 'Don't you drop that hammer now, you hear?'

For a brief moment, Cody couldn't decide whether to fire or flee, and then mercifully something about the startled man seemed familiar. It abruptly dawned on him that he was facing friend, not foe. Groaning with relief, he gently eased down the hammer and holstered his Colt.

His reprieved victim heaved a huge sigh of relief. 'You look like you done seen a ghost, Bill. Just what ails you?'

Cody stared at him for a moment longer, and then his words came in a rush. 'Chuck's swing station got attacked by rebel raiders . . . while I was there. I saw everything, killings an' all. Two Western Union men ran them off in this direction. When I saw no one about, I thought you'd both been kilt for sure. God in heaven, I thought my heart was set to explode!'

Ultimately, he only stopped talking because he'd run out of puff, but that did give his audience a chance to respond. Two of them now stood in the doorway, and one of them couldn't easily forget staring into the muzzle of a Navy Six.

'Land sakes, boy. You done scared the shit out of me, pointing that pistol the way you did!'

It was left to his companion to consider the wider picture. 'Oh, hush up, Jonas. If what Bill here says is true, you might just have way more than that pointing at you afore long.' He stared hard at Cody. 'You say those scavengers were headed this way?'

The courier nodded. 'But they were shot up some.'

'Why in tarnation would Western Union men step in to help the likes of us?' queried Jonas sourly.

His more pragmatic partner came to a decision. 'Who cares? It's the here and now that matters.' Glancing sharply at the new arrival, he commanded, 'Shift your mochila on to that fresh horse and then ride like the devil. Your only responsibility is to get the mail through. If there's some fellas coming here looking for blood, then that's our problem.'

Cody stared at him dumbly.

'*Move*, boy. You ain't too big for me to wup your hide!'

Less than two minutes later, the Pony Express courier was back in the saddle, and again riding west at great speed. He felt a deal of guilt at leaving the two men, but also great relief. He'd been in more than enough gunfights for one day.

Captain Seward lay on the grass next to his enlisted man, a drawtube spyglass to his right eye. On seeing the mail rider racing away, he cursed bitterly. They were just too late to stop him, but on reflection he decided that they'd just have to make the best of it. The most pressing matter was to secure more horses. Killing and robbing the two operators would also give his men some satisfaction, but this time he determined to take no chances. It still rankled that someone had managed to get the drop on him, so on this occasion the Pony Express employees would definitely die, and without even knowing who had murdered them.

By a combination of luck and guile, the captain had managed to obtain a 'top notch' sharpshooter for his raiding party. And this particular sharpshooter came equipped with one of the Confederacy's most prized long-range, muzzle-loading Whitworth rifles. The fledgling nation had managed to purchase around one hundred and fifty of the precision British weapons at the exorbitant cost of one thousand dollars each. And Seward was about to find out just how good they were.

Because of the open ground around the station, the assassin and his assistant were a good six hundred yards away. Due to the reloading time required for using the innovative hexagonal bullet, the marksman needed both men out in the open and away from the cabin. That way the raiders could bag the pair of them without the need for a siege. And it was because the Pony Express employees needed to look after the remounts that gave Seward his opportunity.

'Now's your chance, Teague,' he muttered. 'They're both in the corral, tending to the horses.'

The sharpshooter grunted. 'I see 'em.' Not for the first time the lean, pockmarked specialist neglected to finish with the required 'sir'. He took liberties with his élite status, which his officer was usually prepared to overlook as long as he was successful.

Because they were operating in the field, Teague's rifle did not possess a fragile copper tube scope above the barrel. He had to make do with a ladder sight, but at a 'mere' six hundred yards that would be no problem. As he lined up on the unsuspecting individual carrying a heavy feed sack, the corners of his mouth turned up in a grim smile. He was a man who truly enjoyed his work.

Jonas was rubbing down Cody's tired animal when he perceived a strange, shrill whistling sound, the like of which he'd never heard before. Glancing around, he was surprised to see his partner lying on the ground, legs twitching as though he was having some kind of fit. Jonas's slow wits suddenly recognized the sound of a distant gunshot, and a wave of fear flooded over him.

'Oh Jesus, it's them,' he wailed, his mind in turmoil. Instinctively he knew that his only chance was to reach the cabin before the marksman reloaded, so he made a frantic dash for the corral fence.

As his sharpshooter heaved on the Whitworth's ramrod, Seward hissed, 'Don't fail me, Teague. He's running like a pronghorn buck.'

'Don't fret, cap'n,' the other man retorted. 'He's a dead man.' With the bullet firmly in place, he slipped on a fresh percussion cap, and resumed his prone position. At such a distance, a moving target required real skill, but Teague knew that he was more than equal to the task.

Having literally flung himself over the fence, Jonas was running for his life. As the fast-moving figure careered towards the open door, Teague had to take many factors into account. Distance, speed and direction all came into play, but for him the shot was never in doubt. In fact he deliberately held off a moment longer, to draw out the tension that he knew Seward would be experiencing. Then he fired, and the unusually shaped projectile slammed into his victim's back, just as that man reached the sanctuary of the sod cabin. Coughing blood, Jonas tripped and sprawled headlong on to the hard-packed dirt floor.

'You nearly left that too long, Teague,' Seward accused sharply. He held a vague suspicion that the sharpshooter had toyed with him.

'Just wanted to be sure, *sir*,' the other man retorted, and then couldn't resist adding, 'I reckon it's safe for you all to go over there now.'

Seward's eyes flashed dangerously as he got to his feet. 'Don't test me, soldier. Nobody is irreplaceable.' With that, he strode back to recover his horse.

Teague smirked. He reckoned that one way or another it was going to be a good war!

Cody's new mount had settled nicely into its stride, and the young man's natural confidence was gradually returning. Then suddenly he heard a faint crack somewhere down his back trail. Alarmed, he reined in hard and sat listening. As long seconds passed, all he could discern was his animal's heavy breathing. Then he heard it. Another sharp crack, and this time he knew for sure that it was gunfire.

With beads of sweat beginning to form on his smooth features, the Pony Express courier pondered just what to do next. It didn't take him long. The instructions so recently and forcefully given to him were etched into his mind. His duty was all too clear.

The mail had to get through . . . at least into the hands of the next relay rider. And so it was that William Frederick Cody again turned west, and safely rode off into history.

CHAPTER SIX

Along with pondering their next move, something specific had been troubling Ransom Thatcher ever since the two men had left the Pony Express station.

'You had that bearded bastard under your gun, and yet you didn't kill him. I reckon I need to know why?'

The Texan favoured him with a sidelong glance. With the growing realization that his young companion was actually a pretty sharp cuss, he'd been expecting such a question.

'And I reckon it serves no good purpose to keep it from you. His name's Seward. He served with me in the Mexican War. Seeing him there, large as life, after all these years, kind of unmanned me.'

Despite the disconcerting disclosure, Thatcher was curious. 'In Hays' ranger command?'

Surprisingly, Kirby chuckled. 'Nah. Believe it or not, they'd put us under an Englishman, name of Thomas Collins. Similar in age to you, I guess, and God damn it but he knew how to soldier. We all went ashore at

Vera Cruz, and then moved inland on a special mission. We saw a fearful amount of violence down there. A lot of good men died.'

He went quiet as old memories flooded back, but Thatcher wasn't quite prepared to leave it there. 'And after?'

The former ranger shook his head. 'Kind of lost touch with all of them after Mexico. I'd got tired of killing Comanches, so I left the rangers and began to drift north. There's always work for a man with my skills.'

'And if we catch up with this Seward again, what then?'

Kirby's expression hardened. 'He always was a contrary son of a bitch. If we've ended up on opposite sides, then he'll have to pay the consequences. Would be a shame if I had to kill him though, 'cause he never really did me any harm. But don't go fretting. I won't turn soft on you.' He paused for a moment before adding, 'I may be from the South, but I don't know how this new war's gonna pan out, and I don't really care. I've never kept slaves, and I don't really hold with slavery. All this is just a job of work, but I take my work very seriously.'

Thatcher decided that that was probably about as good a declaration of intent as he could reasonably hope for. As the two men continued steadily north, he determined that it was time to discuss their plans, because he'd been giving their options a lot of thought.

'We know now that the Pony Express had nothing

61

to do with the wrecking and killings. And the tele-graph is a far more important target than the overland mail route. It's the future. If this Seward is going to try again, I reckon he'll have another crack at the repair crews.' He glanced questioningly at Kirby.

'Keep going,' that man responded.

'Which means he'll strike somewhere near Omaha again, so as he doesn't have to wait around too long. Trouble is, there's still an awful lot of territory to cover.'

'Between, say, Omaha and Fremont maybe?' Kirby replied, somewhat mischievously.

'Well, yeah, I guess.'

'But if that city slicker boss of yourn did as you asked,' the older man continued, 'then there might could be some hired help waiting for us in Fremont.'

'So?'

'*So*, we mosey on over there and spread them out north of the line between both towns, and wait for something to happen. As soon as someone spots a big fire, they come full chisel for us, rolling up any of the others on the way.' The Texan stopped and peered at his companion with mock belligerence. 'What do you think to my plan?'

Thatcher laughed. 'I think it might just work.'

Kirby winked. 'Yeah, so do I. Unless, of course, Cornell's left us high and dry. He had the look of a man who might.'

Fremont had the confused, impermanent look of a lot of frontier towns. Unconsciously emulating Omaha, and created purely to cash in on the expected arrival of the Union Pacific Railroad, its rudimentary buildings had been thrown together quickly. Yet until the 'iron horse' actually steamed in, it would depend on Western Union and passing wagon traffic on the Platte River Road for its survival. That situation made Ransom Thatcher a man of some influence, a fact that could prove useful.

'I'm going to check for news in the telegraph office,' he remarked, as the two men rode slowly along Fremont's main, and only dirt thoroughfare. It was the morning after the vicious encounter on the prairie, and after a deal of hard riding, both they and their animals were well used.

'I'll see to the horses in the livery,' Kirby replied. 'And then I'm for the saloon. See what they've got that will cut through the dust.'

It was whilst in the livery that he noticed a number of other horses, far more than he would have expected for such a sleepy settlement. Either Cornell had come good, or there were an unusual number of strangers in town.

With the animals being rubbed down and grain fed, Kirby eagerly made for the only saloon. Hastily constructed out of rough-cut timber, it had little to commend it other than the promise of abundant alcohol. In fact the Texan decided that he had been shot at in better looking places . . . but a drink was a drink!

The single, large room boasted a long counter that almost ran the entire length of one side. It had also once been polished, and had obviously come from some other establishment. A selection of mismatched tables and chairs were strewn around the remaining space. Various kerosene lamps supplemented the light from one grubby window that faced on to the street: out on the frontier, oil was cheaper than panes of glass by far.

A sweaty, bored-looking bartender regarded the new arrival with little interest. With no other competition in town, he had scant need to engage with his customers. Of these, there was a smattering of townspeople, and in one corner a group of eight men. From their noticeably flushed and boisterous demeanour, they had been drinking for some time.

Kirby stood for a long moment, looking them over. If they *had* been sent by Cornell, then they would be of little use to Thatcher drunk. Then again, he decided, it was probably wiser to let his companion challenge them. The young man would be known to them, and besides . . . Kirby had an urgent hankering for some strong drink of his own. He turned eagerly to the counter, unaware that the group had noticed his interest in them.

'Whiskey,' he demanded, and waited impatiently whilst the bartender sauntered over at an insultingly leisurely pace. 'Today would be good,' he added sharply. 'Dawdling service, I don't need!'

The other man glanced at him sourly, and contemplated a tart retort. But something stopped him. He had only survived in this job by being able to recognize trouble. And this grey-haired hombre, with the cold eyes and scarred neck, reeked of it. So instead he kept quiet, and poured out a full measure of house 'rot gut' from a large ceramic receptacle.

'And leave the jug,' Kirby added. It was with the joy of long anticipation that he put the glass to his lips.

'Why was you watching us, old man?'

The harsh voice was slightly slurred and very close. The Texan sighed with disgust, reluctantly lowered his glass and turned to face his interrogator. The man was heavy set, with a face that surely even his mother would have recoiled at. Smallpox scars and rotten teeth were only the half of it.

'Listen, friend,' Kirby began patiently. 'All I want is a quiet drink. I *really* ain't looking for trouble.' Even as he spoke, he realized that a second man had moved up behind the first, whilst their remaining cronies looked on expectantly. Like it or not, trouble was most definitely brewing.

The pockmarked one grimaced. 'I ain't your friend, and you ain't answered my question, *old man!*'

From behind the counter came a hopeful and remarkably optimistic request. 'Do me a favour, fellas,' pleaded the barkeeper. 'Take it outside. It ain't easy getting new furniture in this shit-hole.'

Kirby's response to both men could not have been predicted. Favouring his inquisitor with a wolfish grin, he casually tossed the untouched whiskey into his face. As the startled troublemaker recoiled in surprise, the Texan seized the heavy jug and viciously smashed it into the side of his head. Then, taking a step back from the abruptly legless and whiskey-soaked thug,

Kirby drew and cocked his massive Colt Walker.

As his victim collapsed to the wooden floor, he pointed the gaping muzzle directly at the horrified features of the second man, and spoke loudly, so that all would hear. 'Any of you sons of bitches makes a move, an' I'll turn his head into a canoe!'

A pool of unpleasant-looking urine suddenly mingled with the spilt whiskey on the timber, as the terrified thug showed just how tough he really was. It was into this highly charged atmosphere that Ransom Thatcher strode. As he gazed at the felled and blood-ied man, his eyes widened. Then they took in the others in the corner of the room. It was the one under Kirby's gun who spoke first, and the relief in his voice was pathetically obvious. 'Mister Thatcher! Thank Christ! Where the hell did you spring from?'

Without lowering his weapon, Kirby looked from one to the other and then laughed. 'I might have known this sorry bunch would be working for you.' Finally holstering his Colt, he turned back to the bar and proffered the empty glass. 'Hit me again, barkeep. This *old man* needs a drink, and I seem to have spilt the first one.'

The nine men were congregated around the saloon's corner table. The group consisted of Kirby, Thatcher and seven of Cornell's indifferent hirelings. The eighth lay unconscious in the stables, his head covered by a rudimentary bandage. It was not a good start, and his cronies uneasily regarded the man who had so casually bested him. It was painfully obvious to the

Texan that the superficially tough-looking gang had obviously considered themselves to be something that they patently weren't. That fact didn't bode well if they were to come up against Seward's detachment.

Thatcher kept his voice low as he addressed them all. 'The telegraph is working between here and Omaha. I've had news from Mister Cornell, which could well complicate our task. Apparently there is a large wagon train of fifty families or so, heading this way along the Platte River Road. They're from back east, making for Oregon, and by all accounts their intention is to escape the fighting that's brewing. They mean nothing to Western Union, but they could be a problem.'

'Why?' grunted the sullen and still shaken individual who had faced the Colt Walker's muzzle.

The owner of that same Colt supplied the answer to that: Kirby was casually cleaning under his fingernails with a nipple pick, but he hadn't missed a thing. Without even looking up, he remarked, 'Because they're travelling *above* the Mason Dixon Line, which makes them the enemy of these rebel raiders. If these sodbusters should happen to be in the wrong place at the wrong time, there could be a lot of innocent blood spilt, because that clever cuss Seward might decide to use them for cover.' He paused, and glanced up to make sure that everyone was paying attention. 'So now I want you men mounted up and heading east. Every few miles, one of you drops off to watch the telegraph line. You catch sight of those murdering bushwhackers, you ride back here for help, picking up the others

67

on the way back. And if anyone encounters the wagon train first, they warn them about the rebels. You clear about all this?'

The seven men stared at him stonily for a moment, before looking questioningly at Thatcher. That man was brusque. 'Kirby speaks for me, and I speak for Mister Cornell . . . who'll be paying your wages. So do *exactly* as he says and move out!'

As the seven men trooped out of the saloon, Kirby glanced at him. 'And what are you gonna be doing, *Mister* Thatcher?'

'I reckon we're best off staying near the telegraph office. If the line goes down, we'll know straightaway that something's wrong, and can ride out full chisel to meet the others.'

The Texan's eyes slid inexorably over to the bar. 'I can live with that.'

CHAPTER SEVEN

Captain Jacob Smith gazed off across the seemingly limitless grassland. His attention had just been caught by a distant plume of smoke, and the sight of it was enough to raise the hairs on the back of his neck. Little over half a day's travel out of Omaha, and already something out of the ordinary was giving him cause for concern. Sighing, he twisted in the saddle and gazed back at his 'command'. A long column of wagons stretched away behind him, drawn by teams of oxen. There wasn't a soldier in sight, of course, because Smith's title had no military basis. He was merely the elected captain of a wagon train, but in its own way that was an immense responsibility, because a great many lives depended on his sound judgement.

The settlers in his charge were not just seeking a new life in the west. They were actively escaping from a land that seemed to be descending into madness. And just possibly some of that folly might have caught up with them. Fleetingly, he wished that they were already on the north bank of the Platte, because some-thing told him that this fire could well relate to the Western Union telegraph poles that stretched out endlessly on their right flank.

Catching sight of a mounted, buck-skinned figure, Smith waved for him to come forward. Taylor Shard was the train's requisite guide and scout. Like most such men, he had been a mountain man until more lucrative opportunities had come along. Apparently tough and capable, he exuded an air of calm author-ity. He was also partial to a corncob pipe, and was contentedly drawing on it when he joined his captain.

'Yeah, I seen it,' Shard remarked, before the other man could even say anything. 'Could be almost any-thing. Surveyors for the railroad, Western Union men, Indians. Maybe even secessionist raiders. Now wouldn't that be a thing to write home about, eh?' He glanced at Smith and smiled. 'Reckon you'd like me to find out though, yeah?'

The other man matched his smile. 'I'd be much obliged . . . if it ain't too much trouble.'

The scout swung his horse away, but then contin-ued on so that he executed a full circle. When he again faced the captain, his expression was deadly serious. 'Ain't my place to tell you your job, but if I was you I'd tell those pilgrims to arm themselves. Could be they might just have more than snakes to shoot at.' With that, he again wheeled away and moved off to the west, still puffing on his pipe.

Smith frowned thoughtfully as he watched him leave. He sincerely hoped that it wouldn't come to *any* kind of shooting. Most of his settlers were just farmers and the like, keen to start a new life in the fertile and *peaceful* northwest, well away from the storm brewing back east. Still, any man toting a gun could appear imposing to a possible aggressor, and it was best to be careful. Consciously relaxing his tanned features, Smith headed back to join the approaching wagon train.

Faith Harper watched closely as the train's leader returned. She could never admit it to anyone, married as she was, but she enjoyed observing Jacob Smith. There was something delightfully masculine and reassuring about him, unlike her rather spineless husband. She had only married Joe on the pleading advice of her dying mother, who was desperately fearful that she would end up alone in the world. At the time it hadn't really occurred to the young woman that with her looks she could have held out for someone better.

Now, as she plodded along by the side of the Harper family's wagon, her long dress sweeping through the grass, she instinctively realized that something was bothering the big captain. It secretly pleased her to know that she was very likely the only one to spot it.

Smith raised his hand to halt the 'prairie schooners'. He had already decided not to circle them . . . just yet. An unknown fire was not enough justification for such a manoeuvre, because the whole process would take up altogether too much travelling time. The knowledge that they had to be across the Rockies before the snow arrived was like a nagging toothache that never left him. He would just have to wait on Shard's report first, which would be the hardest part of all this.

Once they had got all the wagons stopped, he rode halfway down the line and yelled his announcement through cupped hands. 'You've probably seen the smoke up ahead. It may be nothing, or it may be something. Either way, I want you to make sure your shooting irons are all loaded and the caps properly seated.' There was a rush of questions from the alarmed settlers, which he completely ignored. 'Whatever transpires, there's to be no shooting without my say so. Not even if you spot a God-damn snake!'

The volume of questions increased, but Smith's only interest was in seeing their guide casually riding back to join them, the corncob pipe clenched between his teeth, and so he urged his mount back to the head of the column. As he rode past the Harpers' wagon, he saw Faith looking up at him.

'My God, but she's a handsome woman,' he thought, and not for the first time. It was only with an effort that he dragged his eyes back to the horizon. 'Come on, Taylor,' he muttered. 'Show yourself.'

Seward watched with satisfaction as the latest batch of severed telegraph poles turned to ashes. Yet he hadn't survived for so long by concentrating on only one thing for too long. His restless eyes were constantly roaming over the terrain, and so it was that he was the first to spot the stranger. Even while pondering the implications, he also took action.

'Teague.'

'Yo.'

'You see that lone rider?'

'I do.'

'If he tries to run, drop him . . . and it wouldn't hurt to say "sir" now and again.'

'Yo.'

Seward sighed. He'd have had any other man bucked and gagged. As it was, he merely returned to scrutinizing the horseman.

As Shard crested the low rise, he happened upon a thoroughly unsettling sight. A large band of bizarrely clad individuals were feeding a massive blaze. Simultaneously, the mountain man recognized the fuel source and noticed that the telegraph line had ceased to exist. This could only be the gang of murdering cut-throats they had been warned about back in Omaha!

Although maintaining steady progress towards them, his mind was turning cartwheels. He had to warn the settlers without leading this mob straight back to them . . . and without getting killed in the process. Mind made up, Shard yanked on the reins, brutally dug in his spurs and raced off to the south.

'Teague?'

That man remained unhelpfully silent. As he carefully sighted down the long barrel of his cherished

Whitworth rifle, the sharpshooter was all the while calculating range and speed. The fleeing man had worked his animal up to quite a pace. The distance was increasing fast, and Teague abruptly came to a decision. Slightly lowering the muzzle, he squeezed the trigger. With a crash, his piece discharged, and the fast-moving horse went down as though tripped by wire. Its rider was flung forward, landing heavily, but recovering with surprising speed.

Miraculously, Taylor Shard came out of the enforced roll in an upright position and then lurched painfully towards his stricken horse. Although in great discomfort, the scout knew exactly what he needed to do. Unsheathing his hunting knife, he steeled himself for the awful task ahead. Ignoring the bulging eyes, Shard sawed through the exposed neck artery, only narrowly avoiding the inevitable geyser of blood. Angrily dropping the fouled knife, he yanked his Spencer from its leather scabbard and dropped down behind the twitching creature. Even as he did so, he heard a strange, shrill whistling sound, and a projectile slammed into the now dead animal.

'Bastard's made himself a fort, cap'n.'

'I can see that,' Seward barked in annoyance, as he slammed shut his drawtube spyglass. It was an unnecessary complication that he could well do without. 'You'll have to stay here until you kill him. . . or at least keep his head down. I need to see whether he was all on his lonesome or not.' Turning to his waiting men, the rebel leader bellowed out, 'Mount up and follow me!'

Jacob Smith heard the two shots with frightening clarity. They were all the more chilling because neither of them came from a Spencer. 'Jesus Christ!' he exclaimed. It was abruptly time to change his mind. 'We've got trouble,' he hollered back. 'Circle the wagons!'

A solid farmer by the name of Jared Buckley sat on the bench seat of the first wagon. For a long moment he just stared in silent horror at the captain.

'Circle the God-damn wagons,' that man angrily repeated. 'Or get to digging graves for you and your woman.'

Now that did get a response, and the first wagon began to swing off to one side, but Smith had an awful feeling they would be too late. He was just about to be proved right.

Seward and his marauders came sweeping in over the low rise. Before them lay a long column of mostly stationary wagons. Only the front one was in motion, its owner frantically whipping the team of four oxen, but to what purpose wasn't clear. Abruptly reining in, the former ranger instinctively sized up the situation, and almost immediately reached a conclusion. A wagon train full of settlers would make perfect cover for his company of raiders. For some time, its planned westward journey would parallel the telegraph line, allowing his men to destroy it wholesale, and all the while they would be able to feed off the 'sodbusters'. After all, he and his men *were* in enemy territory! He almost laughed aloud at the marvellous simplicity of it all.

'Split up down both flanks, and don't shoot anyone unless they resist,' he commanded, and waved his men forward.

Jacob Smith's blood was up, and he had his Colt Navy cocked and ready. He was no stranger to bloody violence, but as he observed the strangely garbed newcomers smoothly split into two groups and make for the wagon train's flanks, he felt his spirits sink. The harsh reality of the situation was inescapable. He recognized that Shard was very likely dead, and that his people were up against professionals. At best, and with a lot of luck, the settlers might shoot a couple of them, but then they would pay with their own lives. Whereas if they didn't resist, then they at least stood a chance of survival.

With a heavy heart, he very reluctantly holstered his revolver and raised his right hand. Urging his horse around, he bellowed down the column, 'Hold your fire. Don't anybody shoot!'

Some ten wagons back from the front, Faith Harper glimpsed the fast approaching horsemen with surprise rather than trepidation, because she really had no idea what was happening. It was only when she saw her husband retract the hammer on his old Springfield muzzleloader that fear entered her thinking.

'Joe!' she cried. 'What are you doing? You heard the captain.'

He barely glanced at her. His thin features were strained and tense. He'd seen her furtive glances in

Smith's direction, and he knew full well that he hadn't ever really enjoyed her full respect. In fact he sometimes wondered why someone with her looks had agreed to marry him at all. This was his chance to prove to his lovely wife just what he was capable of.

Pounding hoofs announced the arrival of the mysterious and suddenly very frightening riders on the flanks of the wagon train. Their clothes were a confusing mixture of drab and garish, and some of the men could have passed for hostile Indians – none of which gave any clue to their real identity. Yet there could be no doubting their hostile intentions. All brandished either long guns or belt guns, and as one of them drew level with his wagon, Joe Harper made his move.

Swivelling on the bench seat, the settler swung his rifle towards the unknown man's chest, and theatrically cried out, 'No drunk fella's going to get his filthy hands on my wife!'

Joe's own hands were trembling violently, but at such point-blank range he just couldn't miss. All he had to do was squeeze the trigger. But as he was suddenly discovering, it's a hell of a thing to take a man's life, and for a brief, fatal moment he hesitated.

There was no such restraint on the part of his intended victim. The horseman spotted the gaping muzzle, and instantly triggered his Remington revolver. The large-calibre ball smashed into Joe Harper's thin face, taking flesh and bone with it, as the abruptly misshapen piece of lead then created a far larger exit wound. Faith screamed as her suddenly

77

unrecognizable husband fell back off the wagon.

As the nearest of their fellow travellers witnessed the shocking death, they were gripped by terrible indecision. Their natural instinct was to help, but none of them were gunfighters, whilst the thugs swarming around them had the appearance of natural-born killers.

Then Captain Smith rode down the line, both hands now held high, followed by the marauders' apparent leader. 'No more shooting,' he cried. 'There's no shame in it. We're outmatched and out-gunned.'

With obvious relief, his people lowered their guns, all the while averting their eyes from Faith Harper's genuinely grievous distress.

Seward nodded with grim satisfaction. 'Mighty sensible of you folks,' he called out. 'You're no use to us dead. All we want is your willing company and hospitality.' His brutalized features creased in the makings of a smile, but it completely failed to reach his eyes. 'And that widow looks fit to be tied. Someone had better tell her not to get any foolish notions.'

Then another gunshot crashed out from over the rise, indicating that Teague hadn't yet settled matters. Seward angrily rounded on the wagon captain. 'Who the hell all is out there?'

Smith regarded the rebel leader with cold loathing. 'I might ask you the same thing, about all of you. I don't recognize any of those uniforms, and those fellas sure ain't like any Indians known to me.'

Seward nodded knowingly, his annoyance abruptly

under control. 'So it's an information exchange, is it? Well OK, I'll go along with that for a *little* while. 'Cause I can see how you could be curious.' He ferociously scratched his bearded chin for a moment before continuing. 'This is how it is. You're all now prisoners of war of the Confederacy. I'm sure you've probably heard of us. But here's the thing. We ain't really interested in any of you folks, but we do need your co-operation. So anyone does anything to hinder us, any little thing at all, and they're a dead man.' His glance settled on Faith Harper's tear-stained face, and he menacingly added, 'Or woman! Savvy?'

Smith's eyes widened at such unexpected revelations, and his right hand instinctively drifted towards his holstered Colt. The furtive move was not missed by the sharp-eyed rebel. 'Now you look like a man who could be trouble, but I'll allow that I've given you plenty to think on, an' not all of it good. So here's what's gonna happen. I want every weapon on this wagon train in a pile here, at my feet. Then we're gonna load the whole lot into the back of one wagon, which will then be off limits to all of you. But first off, you need to tell me whose horse we shot out from under him. Or that grieving widow will be joining her husband!'

The wagon captain glanced at Faith's anguished but still beautiful face, and he knew that he really didn't have any choice. 'He's an old-time mountain man by the name of Taylor Shard,' he reluctantly replied. 'Works for us as hunter and guide both. And from what I've seen, he sure can shoot.'

As if to emphasize that fact, yet another shot sounded off. Seward stared hard at him for a moment and then sighed. 'Is that a fact?' Glancing over at one of his men, he instructed, 'Take Decker with you and see what's keeping Teague. It doesn't normally take him this long to kill a man. If he needs help, give it!' Returning his attention to Smith, he remarked, 'I sure hope you've got someone else who knows the way!'

Taylor Shard cursed as another bullet whistled in like a mountain howitzer. The lead buried itself deep in the inert body of his horse. 'Just he's already dead,' he bellowed sarcastically over to the increasingly frustrated marksman.

Not that the besieged guide really had anything to crow about. He was effectively pinned down and helpless, until the other marauders inevitably returned to finish him off. His opponent knew his business. Hidden in deep grass, he appeared to shift position after each shot. Shard's only consolation was that with his new Spencer repeater, he would be able to sell his life dearly. Not that he had any desire to die just yet. Then he heard the sound that he had been dreading. From off to his right, he heard the noise of pounding hoofs. It appeared that he had a proper fight on his hands!

CHAPTER EIGHT

'The God-damn line's down again,' Thatcher bellowed, as he barged into Fremont's saloon.

Kirby glanced over at him with mild disappointment. It was a fact that after a couple of drinks, the local 'bug juice' actually became almost palatable. *Almost.* 'Between here and Omaha?' It was really more of a statement than a question.

'Uhuh,' grunted the younger man.

Unusually for him, Kirby became almost philosophical. 'So much for sleeping on a genuine mattress tonight. But hell, it's probably ticky anyhu.' Glancing at the bartender, he added, 'I'll be back, so don't go hiding that jug, you hear?'

Some ten minutes later, the two men were saddled up and heading east out of town. They were travelling fast. Too fast really, but they were very conscious of the sun going down behind them.

'D'you really think those sons of bitches we sent looking will have actually split up?' Kirby hollered across at his partner.

That required little consideration. 'Nah,' Thatcher grunted. 'I reckon not. And the thought that those settlers might run into Seward's scum-bellies troubles me something awful.'

'Best not to think on it,' the Texan opined. 'It sure won't help any, and it could just get you killed!'

Decker and his companion had carefully moved in behind Teague, leading their animals on foot for the final few yards, and now regarded the prone sharpshooter with particularly bleak amusement. Neither of them had any liking for the man. They considered that his particularly lethal talent allowed him to take way too many liberties with the captain.

'Not finished him off yet, then,' Decker remarked casually, hoping to startle the rifleman.

Teague, who had just finished reloading his piece, and was sweating from the effort involved, knew full well that they were there and so didn't even trouble to turn around. 'If Seward's sent you over,' he snarled. 'It's because he wants to be on his way and you're here to *assist* me. So that's just what you're gonna do. That cockchafer over yonder is forted up and keeping his head down. He could even be asleep,' he added, with an uncharacteristic attempt at humour. 'You'll have to flush him out for me. Mount up and ride out a-ways, one on each side of me, and then rush him. I'll guarantee your miserable hides, 'cause if he shows himself, I *will* nail him.'

The two men, both wearing grubby, ill-fitting grey uniforms, regarded him dubiously. 'That ain't much of a plan,' Decker finally commented.

Teague spat a stream of chewing tobacco into the grass. 'It's the best you're getting. Now move ... unless you want me to tell the cap'n you refused.'

The other two frowned unhappily, but since neither of them fancied being shot in the foot, they really didn't have any choice. Backing off slightly, they reluctantly mounted up. 'If we've got to do this, we'd better do it properly, 'cause it's our skins,' muttered Decker. 'Move out about fifty yards, then when I signal go full chisel for that bastard. Yeah?'

The other man nodded his assent, and that was exactly what they did.

Seward watched with satisfaction as the last of the firearms were loaded into the designated wagon. The weapons took the place of a pile of furniture, now discarded next to the wagon, and the sight of its distraught owners vaguely amused him. They were bitterly upset that it was to be left behind ... but not enough to want to fight about it. Faith Harper, however, was a different proposition.

'Let's move 'em out,' barked the rebel leader. 'I want to put some distance between us and the fire before nightfall.' He was about to mount up when a shrill voice stopped him.

'What about my husband, you murdering varmint?' she yelled from beside the corpse. 'I can't just leave him here for the vultures. He needs to be buried, and words said over him.'

Seward regarded her with more than casual interest.

His eyes hungrily ran up and down the curves of her body. They took in the lustrous dark hair, good teeth and unblemished skin. Even flushed with anger, she was quite obviously a real peach. And yet he didn't really have time for such distractions. 'He called it, lady,' he retorted. 'Shouldn't have drawn down on one of my men. And I ain't got time for this shit, so he stays where he lays!'

Faith angrily shook her head. 'So let me stay behind to dig a grave. I'll catch up after I've finished.'

Seward laughed out loud. 'You must take me for some kind of jackass. The only way you leave this train is feet first, like your man. So don't tempt me!' Considering the matter concluded, he turned away to face his horse – and was therefore surprised at the rush of footsteps behind him.

The startled Confederate officer twisted around, right hand snaking towards his holstered revolver, only to receive a stinging open-handed slap on the face. As a number of his men sniggered at the entertaining sight, Seward drew back his clenched fist . . . and suddenly found it seized in an iron grip. Jacob Smith, although now unarmed, had nevertheless moved up to support Faith.

With great difficulty, Seward controlled the rage that was coursing through his body, and, after glancing meaningfully at his men, settled his hard eyes on the wagon captain. 'So that's how it is, eh? We kill the husband, and you step in. Well, I can't say as I blame you, but if you don't back off pronto, you're gonna end up just like him.' As if to emphasize his threat, there were multiple metallic clicks from around them, as a number of firearms were cocked.

Remarkably, Smith maintained his grip and held his ground. 'You don't want to kill me, captain,' he softly responded. 'You need me to run the wagon train and keep the settlers in line. So how about a little compromise that keeps everyone happy? Let me put her man in the back of their wagon, so that at least we can bury him when we stop for the night.'

With divine timing, another gunshot crashed out over the rise, momentarily diverting Seward's attention. By the time he refocused on Smith, he had lost interest in such trivia. 'OK, OK. If you want him that badly, take him,' he replied, wrenching his fist from the other man's grip. 'But if you ever lay your hands on me again, I'll kill you!' With that, he twisted away and leapt into the saddle. 'Now get these God-damn wagons moving,' he yelled.

Smith bellowed over to Jared Buckley on the lead wagon. 'You heard the man, get going.' Then he turned to Faith, and remarked far more gently, 'Let me help you with Joe.'

The young widow stared at him for a moment, and then fleetingly ran a hand over his right arm before returning to her wagon. She had said not a word, but that brief touch had created a glow in Jacob Smith that was far hotter than any rebel bonfire.

Taylor Shard had glimpsed the arrival of the two reinforcements, and immediately knew what that meant: 'Those bastards are gonna be down my throat any time now,' he muttered to his unresponsive horse. And sure enough, after a brief discussion, he saw them split up and head off in opposite directions. With a sharpshooter just itching to blow his head off, Shard couldn't afford to show himself, and yet somehow he had to defend both flanks at once.

Most other men would have felt the icy grip of panic, but he'd been in tight spots before, and well knew that he couldn't afford to scare. An old-timer had once said to him, 'Don't ever scare, boy. 'Cause if you do, you're dead for sure!'

Knowing that the sharpshooter was unlikely to fire his single shot until his men had flushed out their prey, Shard risked a swift glance around one side of his 'barricade'. For a man of his experience it was enough, and told him all that he needed to know. In spite of their best efforts, one of the riders seemed likely to reach him ever so slightly before the other. It wasn't much, but it gave him an edge of sorts.

Taking a deep breath to steady himself, the scout drew and cocked his Colt Navy, and placed it on the grass. Then he rolled over, and curled up against the belly of his animal, clutching his carbine. Even with a repeater, he would only get the time for one shot with it. The sound of pounding hoofs drummed in his ears, as both assailants swept in at great speed.

And then they were upon him . . . or rather one of them was. A shot crashed out, but the uniformed rider was attempting to both control his mount and shoot. The ball tore into the ground mere inches from Shard's belly, as he took a far more controlled aim at the looming figure. His Spencer literally belched forth death, as the heavy calibre bullet smashed into the man's chest, lifting him out of the saddle.

Dropping the carbine like a hot coal, Shard twisted like an eel to reach his Colt. His fingers closed around it just as the second horseman reached him. This time the two shots were so close that they could have been one, and the muzzle flashes seemed to mingle. A terrible burning sensation lanced into the mountain man's left arm, but all his concentration remained on his opponent. That luckless individual had taken the ball in his right thigh, and was howling with pain even as he tried to control his rearing animal.

It was then that Shard made his only mistake. Recognizing that he had merely wounded his opponent, and fired up for the kill, he rose up slightly to get a better shot. The rebel known as Decker momentarily had his back to the cursed Yankee, who didn't hesitate: discharging his Colt Navy for a second time, he managed to place the .36 calibre ball squarely between Decker's shoulder blades. A burst of exhilaration flowed through Shard – before the shock of realizing that he was no longer hidden from the sharpshooter!

The strangely shaped lead projectile struck him just as he was dropping back down behind his fleshy parapet. A blinding flash erupted through his skull, and all the strength in his body dissipated. With a terrible moan, he toppled forwards on to the grass, and then all was darkness.

*

The long wagon train snaked over the rise and on towards Teague's position. His commander had witnessed the bloody little fight, and was far from happy. He glanced over at Jacob Smith, who had returned to the van after assisting Faith. 'Seems like you were right,' he grimly commented. 'That cockchafer *did* know how to handle himself.'

Smith could have said any number of things, but chose instead discretion, and remained silent. He was seething at the apparent death of his guide, and besides, he was viewing for the first time the wholesale destruction of the telegraph line. It began to dawn on him that their captors weren't just a gang of looters. They had actually come north as part of a planned military campaign to make war on the Union.

Teague had cautiously got to his feet by the time his leader reined in next to him. 'That could have panned out better,' the captain drily remarked. 'He dead, or what?'

The marksman frowned. He didn't enjoy having his specialist skill doubted. 'I got him, *sir*. I know I did.'

'You certain enough to ride on over there on your lonesome and check him out?'

Teague was uncharacteristically silent.

'Hmm, it's like that, is it?' Seward chided, obviously enjoying the other's discomfort. He would happily have carried on baiting the other man for a while longer, but there just wasn't the time. 'Well, you did hit him, an' that's no error, so I guess we'll just leave him to bleed out. No sense in risking any more lives. Two dead is more than enough, and even if he's able, he sure ain't gonna shoot at his own wagon train. Mount up and follow me,' he added dismissively, and with that, he swung away to rejoin the plodding wagons, leaving the chastened enlisted man to follow on.

And yet Teague didn't immediately do so, because even despite the obvious danger and the orders to the contrary, professional pride sorely tempted the marksman to administer a *coup de grace*. Glancing back, his eyes lingered on the fight scene as he battled conflicting emotions.

Unsurprisingly, Ezra Cornell's seven gun thugs were still together. Their progress from Fremont had been unhurried, and since none of them had fancied passing a lonely night on the prairie, they had decided to ignore the belligerent old bastard's instructions . . . at least until daybreak. Six of them were clustered around a small cooking fire, whilst somewhere in the dark the seventh noisily relieved himself. It wasn't long before that individual was back, his return speeded up by more than just a desire for hot coffee.

'There's a whole bunch of campfires off to the east,' he breathlessly reported. 'Could be it's those fellas we're looking for,' he added, somewhat unnecessarily.

That got everybody's full attention. One-sided gunplay was always acceptable, but only so long as the numbers were in *their* favour. 'That makes everything a whole lot easier,' one of his cronies responded. 'Come sun-up, we'll go take a look-see, and then draw straws for who reports back to Thatcher and that Texan prick.'

It was full dark when he at last came to, and for a brief moment the disorientated mountain man actually believed that he was dead. Then the awful, throbbing agony started in his head, and he uttered a loud groan. Cautiously he rolled over, and promptly regretted it. The pounding increased and suddenly he was bathed in sweat. For what seemed like an age, Taylor Shard just lay in the grass with his eyes closed, waiting for the pain to ease.

Very gradually, his misery seemed to decrease, until at length he felt about ready to sit up. Then, from very close by, there came the sound of movement, and any discomfort was suddenly irrelevant. Ignoring the renewed torture, he desperately scrabbled around in the grass searching for a firearm. Whoever it was had to be almost upon him. Just when he thought he would have to resort to the knife in his belt, Shard's right hand patted a cold, hard surface – and abruptly the Colt was in his grasp.

With two chambers already discharged, and one always kept empty under the hammer, he therefore had three available. After cocking the gun under his buckskin jacket, he fell back against the distended belly of his horse, eyes straining for the source of the noise. When he finally spotted it in the gloom, Shard could have wept with relief.

'Sweet Jesus!' he exclaimed. 'You damn near ended up like your compatriot here.'

The horse innocently ambled into view and nickered quietly, as though sensing the human's anxiety. It had once belonged to the Pony Express, before being stolen by Seward's men. With its new owner lying dead in the grass, it had galloped off in fear, before slowly returning in search of company. Although scaring Shard half to death, the animal's arrival meant that he now had the means to follow the wagon train. But first he had other matters to attend to.

He was hurting from the wounds he had received, but thankfully both were superficial. His left arm had lost some flesh and had bled for a time into his cotton shirt, and then the whole mess had dried together. Separating the two proved to be exquisitely painful, but finally, using water from his canteen, he achieved it. By tearing a piece of material from his only spare shirt, he was then able to bandage it.

The scout had been incredibly lucky with the head wound. By touch alone, he gingerly discovered that the bullet had merely creased his skull. Dried blood coated his face, but after washing that off, Shard decided to leave the superficial injury to its own devices. Only then did he approach his new mount. The creature was biddable enough, allowing him to remove the saddle and replace it with his own. Dragging that from under a dead weight was by far the hardest part of the task.

Finally, with his firearms reloaded and a mouthful of delicious pemmican to chew on, he moved off on foot, leading his four-legged replacement. Unlike a lot of folks, he had no fears about travelling at night, and in any case was keen to get well clear of the assorted cadavers before they really began to turn. He also had a far bigger incentive. At some point during the murderous little shindig, his well travelled corncob pipe had been irreparably crushed. That son-of-a-bitch sharpshooter had a lot to answer for!

CHAPTER NINE

As they tried to make sense of the drastic change in their circumstances, a desperate uneasiness had settled like a cloying fog over the settlers. It was hard to accept that they were now, in effect, prisoners of war, in an internecine conflict they wanted no part of. The wagon train had camped for the night between the Platte River and an undamaged section of Western Union telegraph poles: these were set to be the intended targets for the next morning. As usual, the wagons were circled, but nothing else about the encampment was normal. Settlers and Confederates had built separate campfires, but that did nothing to ease the tension. Seward had demanded that his men be fed; yet now that they had been, the thoughts of some of their number were on other, less savoury matters.

There were plenty of full-grown women amongst the party, but many were plain and all were married ... with the exception of Faith Harper. It was obvious for all to see that she was neither of those things, and as she sat, brooding and alone by her wagon, some of the marauders began to nudge each other suggestively. Jacob Smith, having laboured hard to carve a grave out of the unyielding prairie, was down by the river washing the sweat from his body. The opportunity that certain individuals had been hoping for came when their captain strolled off to inspect the doomed telegraph line – and of course the instigator had to be Teague.

'That little filly looks kind of lonesome, moping over her husband and thinking on what she's missing,' he remarked lasciviously. 'What say we sashay over there and show her a good time?'

'Yeah, it was good of Butler to kill him for us,' another chuckled. 'What with her being such a handsome woman, an' all.'

Strangely, Joe Harper's killer was far from enthusiastic. 'It was him or me, an' I don't regret it, but it don't seem right going after his widow. Just 'cause she's a Northerner don't make her evil or some such.'

The sharpshooter had little time for such nonsense. 'Fine. You stay here and polish your pistol, while we see to business!' With that, he got to his feet and nodded at his other three like-minded cronies. Together they moved expectantly towards the Harper wagon.

'The captain ain't gonna like this,' the dissenter called after them, prompting Teague to call back, 'The hell with him. He ain't here, an' I got an itch that needs scratching!'

The four men's purposeful approach was not

missed by some of the many settlers, congregated uneasily around their cooking fires. Big Jared Buckley flushed angrily, and moved to intercept them, but his wife, scrawny yet determined, barred his way. She was motivated by a mixture of common sense and more than a little envy. No gang of lustful marauders had their eyes set on her! 'Don't be a dang lame brain, Jared,' she hissed. 'Thanks to Jacob Smith, we haven't got a gun between us, and she ain't worth it anyway. If you go over there, they'll kill you, sure as shooting, and then there'll be another widow in the camp!'

With genuine reluctance, he allowed himself to be dissuaded. And so it was with the other menfolk. Since none of them were gunfighters, they had all persuaded themselves that Joe Harper had therefore been a pure fool to draw down on the raiders.

The real target of all this attention, unhappily caught up in a host of thoughts of her own, was completely oblivious to all the fuss. It wasn't until the four men had formed a semi-circle around her that Faith registered their unwelcome presence. For a moment she uncomprehendingly stared up at them from beside her fire. Then her startled gaze took in their blatant scrutiny of her body, and a shock of fear swept through her.

'Yeah, that's right, little lady,' Teague menacingly began. 'We've come for a visit. The captain said how you should give us your willing company, so let's get to it.'

'She looks better than any twenty dollar whore I've ever seen,' muttered one of his companions. To his mind, such an observation was a glowing compliment.

The four men held off for a few seconds longer, as they licked their lips in anticipation. Momentarily frozen with terror, she could do no more than stare at them, her eyes as wide as saucers. Then, as though released from a cage, they went for her like rabid dogs. Such brutal behaviour obviously wasn't new to them, because they tackled her with practised speed. Two grabbed an arm each, whilst a third seized her ankles. She just managed to unleash a piercing scream, before Teague slapped a horny hand over her mouth, and then the gang heaved her bodily into the back of her wagon.

By a lucky coincidence, Faith landed unhurt on her own bed, but as her attackers bundled in after her under the canvas cover, the young woman's prospects were dire. As though acknowledging Teague's ascendancy, the others merely held her down, allowing him free rein to delve under her skirts in the semi-darkness.

'Please!' she howled desperately. 'Don't do this!'

Any further protests were curtailed by a vicious backhanded slap that left her ears ringing and her eyes watering. The casual violence only inflamed them more, and with his knees firmly between her creamy thighs, the sharpshooter was entirely consumed by lust. He wouldn't have detected a stampede, and so certainly didn't hear the rapid footsteps coming up behind him. A powerful hand reached in, grabbed Teague by the throat and hauled him backwards out of the wagon, before dropping him on to the grass. As he lay there, momentarily helpless and with his legs conveniently wide apart, Jacob Smith ferociously slammed his right boot into a satisfyingly unprotected groin.

The wave of agony that flowed through the would-be rapist defied all description. Teague wasn't even able to cry out. All he could do was curl up into a foetal ball, leaving him as vulnerable as a baby. Smith would happily have continued his assault, except that Faith wasn't yet safe and there were others to contend with. He turned just in time to face another of the gang, as that individual leapt out of the wagon. Reacting fast, Smith stepped aside and smashed his left fist into the man's stomach. Then, pivoting on his left foot, he swung around and delivered a perfect haymaker to his victim's jaw.

'Watch out,' Faith yelled, alerting him to the next challenge.

The remaining pair had the sense to work together. One of them clambered out, whilst the other remained in the wagon and drew a belt gun. Smith had no choice. Charging towards him, he knocked the revolver aside, and then struck him a glancing blow across the face. Sadly, in doing so, he left himself open to the fourth man. The wagon captain paid for that with a solid punch to the belly that sent him down to his knees. Although winded and in pain, he still somehow anticipated his assailant's next move, and reached out to intercept a ferocious kick.

The man in the wagon angrily wiped blood from his mashed lips and again took aim at their persistent foe.

Dancing shadows from the flickering flames meant that he had to concentrate that bit harder. But just as he was on the point of squeezing the trigger, two clawed hands seized his lank, greasy hair and pulled hard. The sudden pain in his scalp was intense. As he fell back, his forefinger contracted and a muzzle flash briefly flared in the night.

Momentarily, everyone involved in the desperate struggle froze. By now the whole camp was aware of what was taking place. Amazingly, the remaining Confederate soldiers were content to keep a wary eye on the settlers, and merely viewed the desperate fight as light entertainment. None of them had any great regard for the sharpshooter, and many gave a sly smile as they watched Teague battle with the continuing agony in his groin. But then their captain returned, and abruptly everything changed.

Another, even louder gunshot crashed out, and this time the ball struck earth between Jacob Smith and the man whose foot he was wrestling with. Again, both of them froze, and then Faith's rescuer reluctantly released his hold on the worn leather boot. In the wagon, she continued to retain her tenacious grip on the clumps of unwashed hair, until an elbow jabbed sharply into her ribs. Groaning, her fingers reflexively untwined and he was finally free.

'You bitch!' howled her attacker. He unleashed a tremendous backhand slap, and would have gone on to do a great deal more, if his furious officer hadn't suddenly reached in and dragged him over to the rear of the wagon.

'You worthless scum,' Seward railed at him. 'We're here to make *war* on the Union, not rape their women!' He glanced down at the still hurting Teague. 'I might have known you'd be involved in this!'

For once the overconfident sharpshooter just couldn't manage any kind of reply, and so his commanding officer turned his attention to the wagon train's captain. Seward's massive 'horse pistol' was vaguely pointing in his direction. 'You're sorely testing me, mister, but I've got to admit that keeping four of them off that woman was no mean feat. Still, by rights I ought to kill you for it, but then I might just need you tomorrow. So I'm gonna put you in irons instead.' Turning to his ranking non-com, he added, 'See to it, sergeant. And then you can tell me why you didn't attempt to stop all this.'

That man coloured under the sudden scrutiny, and quickly busied himself with his new prisoner. His abrupt desire for obscurity was aided by Faith Harper's appearance at the rear of the wagon. She was still dazed from the last blow, and blood trickled from the corner of her mouth. Unbeknown to her, with her clothes torn and in disarray, a great deal more flesh was on show than was proper.

To men short on female company, she made a distractingly alluring sight. Seward's hungry eyes took in the impressive cleavage, and he felt a sudden empathy with the four would-be rapists. Then he remembered why they were there, and guilty anger surged through him. 'Fix yourself, woman,' he barked. And then, peering around at all those looking on, both

Confederates and settlers alike, he added 'Get back to your business, all of you. This ain't some bordello.'

As the watching crowd reluctantly broke up, and Smith was led away to be fitted with manacles, Faith called out. 'Thank you, Captain . . .' She paused deliberately as both men glanced back at her. Only then did she finish. '*Smith*. I won't forget this!'

The wagon train captain smiled. Somehow he was sure that *he* wouldn't, either!

Cornell's seven hired hands regarded the circled wagon train pensively. It was barely first light, but the men had been up and about for some time. The large party of settlers intrigued them. They had already decided that the two gunshots must have been 'joy firing', because there was no sign of trouble, just smoke from the various cooking fires. Only six of them would be going in, because they hadn't recalled their boss's instructions correctly, and thought that they should report their discovery.

'If we tell 'em we're working for Western Union, we might get a good breakfast out of them,' one of them considered.

'Yeah, and a party that size must have some young women. We might just get lucky as well,' another added with undue optimism.

The strangely carefree mood was momentarily dampened by the luckless individual who had drawn the short straw to return to Thatcher. 'Huh, with your luck it'll be salt pork and rock-hard biscuits,' he crowed, 'and all the women'll be dried out spinsters, two years older than God!'

'You're just a sore loser, Shadrach,' yet another commented. 'Best be on your way, afore the cooking smells reach you.'

Shadrach muttered some vague obscenity, before turning to the west and leading his horse away. He presumed that he would be riding back to Fremont, which meant another encounter with that cold-eyed Texan. Cursing his luck, he finally mounted up and rode on, but his lack of enthusiasm meant that his pace was slow. His companions had set off in the other direction with considerably more eagerness. But then some strange sixth sense brought him to a halt. With an uncommon glimmer of intelligence, he decided that it might be better to wait and see how his companions were received. That way, when he did meet up with Thatcher, he would have something more solid to impart. Nodding happily at his own display of initiative, he steered his horse around to retrace its steps.

'There's riders coming in, captain.'

Seward cursed. He had been just about to order the destruction of another stretch of telegraph poles. 'So who the hell are they? Army, Indians, what?' he demanded testily.

'Six men, sir. Look like civilians, but I guess they could be anything,' was the unhelpful response.

The Confederate officer sighed, before calling out to his sergeant. 'I want all the men under cover, now. Spread them around the wagons . . . and release that wagon captain and send him to me. Nobody shoots without my say so.'

Moments later, Jacob Smith arrived at his side, rue-fully rubbing his wrists. By then, Seward had removed his hat and uniform tunic. The big Colt was tucked in his belt behind his back. 'You do the talking,' he ordered calmly. 'Get rid of them without raising their suspicions. That way there won't need to be any killing . . . and remember, we've got all the guns. So don't try any tricks, or you won't see that pretty little widow again.'

Smith stiffened with annoyance, but remained silent. He didn't care for such talk, possibly because he was actually living in hope. His wife had been a long time dead, and she had been a hard act to follow . . . until now!

As the six men arrived before the circled wagons, they should by rights have been searching for any-thing out of the ordinary, but sadly all they had on their minds were food and women. Reining in expec-tantly, they saw two men walking towards them, both apparently unarmed.

'Howdy do, fellas?' one of the newcomers called out. 'Saw your smoke from a ways back. Thought we might share a pot of coffee with you, and maybe some grub if you can spare it.'

'Well, I'm right sorry, friend,' Smith responded with apparently genuine regret. 'I'd like to oblige you, I really would. Only the thing is, we're all packed up and ready to go. We've got a lot of distance to cover today.'

'Your fires are still lit,' came the disappointed and

slightly belligerent retort.

'Just about to kick 'em out,' the wagon captain countered. 'Then Mister Buckley here is going to lead us off. Ain't that so, Mister Buckley?'

Jared Buckley nodded uncomfortably. He had a feeling that something awful was going to happen, and he was right in the middle of it.

None of the horsemen appeared ready to depart, and it was then that Seward entered the conversation. 'Who are you fellas, anyhow? We've been told to be careful out here, what with Indians and road agents and such.'

Belated understanding dawned on the new arrivals. 'Aw hell, you don't need to worry your head about us, mister. We don't mean you no harm. We work for Western Union Telegraph. We're on a special mission,' he added self-importantly.

There was a moment's silence as Seward digested that. Then his hard features lit up in the semblance of a smile. 'Well, why didn't you say that before? We ain't gonna turn law-abiding citizens away, are we? Come right on in, and welcome.' So saying, he stepped up level with Smith, and flashed a warning glance at him.

With childlike eagerness, Cornell's men dismounted and led their animals through the narrow gap between two wagons. They completely failed to notice the grim expression on Buckley's big face. It was only once they were within the circle that certain things began to trouble them.

'What are them pants you're wearing?' one of them asked Seward curiously. 'Looks akin to some kind of uniform, though for the life of me I can't recall seeing their like before.'

Then another one, glancing around at the numerous horses, added, 'You got an awful lot of prime horseflesh, friend. Surely these can't all be saddle horses.'

Seward abruptly raised his right hand in a great sweeping gesture, as though about to provide an explanation. Then he bellowed out, 'Blast 'em!' and threw himself at Smith. Together they tumbled heavily to the ground, just as a ragged volley of shots rang out.

With all hell braking loose around them, the Western Union employees stood no chance whatsoever. A terrible selection of hot lead tore into the startled group. Three of them died instantly, blood pumping profusely from numerous shot holes. The others, although all wounded, managed to draw their weapons, but didn't really have any clear targets to shoot at. Clouds of acrid smoke hung around the canvas wagon hoods, and women and children screamed with fear. Many of them couldn't really comprehend what was happening. Then the Confederate raiders concealed in their midst unleashed a second deafening fusillade, and the massacre was almost complete. With not a man left standing, the guns fell reluctantly silent. For a lot of the attackers, the wholly one-sided engagement had been disappointingly short.

Captain Seward got to his feet, pulled the Colt Walker from behind his back, and calmly strolled over to inspect the slaughter. To his surprise, there was one survivor. The stricken, blood-spattered man was suffering grievous pain, yet still had his wits about him. Gazing up at Seward, his eyes narrowed as he uttered just one word: 'Why?'

Seward pondered that for a moment, then cocked his massive weapon and aimed it at the other's tortured features. 'The South's survival,' he emphatically responded, and then fired. His victim barely had the chance to register bewilderment, before his features were utterly destroyed.

The Confederate officer glanced at each of the other five corpses, before nodding with satisfaction. 'Secure their horses,' he demanded of his emerging men, 'and then break out the tools. We've got some more telegraph poles to burn.'

Jacob Smith stared at him with barely concealed loathing. 'What about these poor creatures? Ain't you even going to give them a Christian burial?'

Seward appeared momentarily puzzled by such a question. 'I reckon not. You've done enough grave digging for this trip, an' wood's not the only stuff that'll burn!'

CHAPTER TEN

Unbeknown to all those within the circled wagons, two other men had each separately witnessed the atrocity.

Initially stunned by the volume of gunfire, Shadrach now stared in total disbelief at the sight of the distant carnage. Although unable to make out the individual bodies, there was absolutely no doubt in his mind about what had just happened. Beads of sweat broke out on his face, as he realized just how close he had come to being a part of it. The difference between life and death had literally come down to the length of a piece of grass. And even though in a state of shock, he knew that now he had to hightail it fast, before the killers noticed his presence. Unexpectedly, the ride back to Fremont no longer seemed like the poorer option. Gratefully turning his horse away, he again headed west – only this time he had some real news to impart.

Taylor Shard lay in the long grass with his newly acquired animal. The weight of his upper body was over the neck of the creature, pinning it reluctantly to the ground. They were on the south-eastern side of the encampment. Although his head was still aching abominably, he had been able to take a far less emotional assessment of the slaughter than was the case with Shadrach, because as far as he could make out through his drawtube spyglass, no one of his acquaintance had been involved in it – in fact, he had no idea who any of the victims were. But from his detached position and with the help of the spyglass, he had also spotted the lone figure in the distance.

Lowering the glass, he nodded grimly and began to ponder his situation. There had been little point in his getting involved in the sudden outbreak of violence, as it would have ended with his death, for sure. And yet he had a duty to help Jacob Smith and the settlers in any way that he could. The hurried westward departure of the solitary horseman allowed for the possibility that he had gone for help. And if that were the case, then Shard might be able to join forces with whoever turned up. Until then, all he could really do was shadow the wagon train and its new masters, all the while watching for an edge or opportunity. The possible outcome, if no help arrived, really didn't bear thinking about.

Ransom Thatcher and Kirby had been travelling steadily east all morning. They had resisted the temptation to push their animals hard, because neither man knew what they might have to face. And since all conversation had long since dried up, the younger man had finally decided that it was high time he asked a certain question.

'If we're riding together, it's only right that I know your given name. So come on, what is it?'

Kirby gazed at him in surprise, before grunting non-committedly. 'Don't see the need, myself. If someone tries to take your life, just holler "Kirby", an' I'll know who you mean.'

Taken aback and intrigued in equal measure, Thatcher sighed and tried again. 'We've fought side by side, and likely there's more killing to come. I deserve to know a little about you, in case I have to dig your grave one day. Wouldn't be right, not to leave a marker.'

Now that tickled the former ranger. 'Huh, that's a mighty cheerful thought. You're a real push-hard, ain't you?'

'So?' Thatcher persisted.

'All right, all right, but there's not much to tell, 'cause the simple fact is I don't *have* another name. My folks were kilt by Comanches, down in West Texas, *before* I could be christened. They were pretty much the earliest American settlers down there, when that area was still owned by Spain, and they certainly didn't deserve to be butchered. Anyhu, after that, most everyone simply called me Kirby, including the people that raised me, and I never gave it any mind. And of course, that's why I joined a ranger company when I was barely off the teat. I wanted revenge, powerful bad. An eye for an eye, a tooth for a tooth, they call it.'

Thatcher was momentarily lost for words. He didn't

consider such a story 'not much to tell'! Curiosity aroused, he had more questions – but before he could continue, Kirby had one of his own. 'Ain't that one of those meat-heads that work for you? He sure looks flustered.'

The other man stared hard, his companion's colourful past abruptly forgotten. 'Damn right it is. He goes by the name of Shadrach. Not the brightest star in the sky,' he added drily.

Spurring their horses forward, it wasn't long before the two men met the greatly relieved messenger. Both horse and rider were lathered up and gasping.

'You look like you done seen a ghost,' the Texan remarked, as Shadrach got his breath.

That man stared wide-eyed at him for a moment. 'Happen you're right,' he finally managed. 'After this day's work.' Then something occurred to him, and he added, 'How come you're way out here, and not in Fremont?'

'The line's down again,' Thatcher briskly replied. 'What did you just mean by that, anyhow? And where's the rest of your cronies?'

Shadrach noisily blew his cheeks out, as though imitating a horse. 'Last I saw of them, they were all shot to hell an' dying.' Before his startled audience could comment, he drew in a deep breath and continued. 'We happened on the circled wagon train. All looked peaceful and we fancied some grub. I drew the short straw, thank Christ, otherwise I wouldn't even be here.'

Kirby peered at him with obvious disgust. 'And I'll

wager it wasn't just the prospect of food that appealed, either. Because instead of thinking with your heads, and sending one man in first, to check it out, all you others rode straight into a trap.' Turning to his companion, he added, 'I guess Cornell's saved on wages, but that don't help us none. For what we need to do, we could have used some extra guns.'

Shadrach stared at him in abject horror. 'Whaaat! You ain't thinking on going back there, are you?'

It was Thatcher who answered that. 'Of course we are, because we're here and there's no one else. These raiders are going to systematically destroy the telegraph line unless we stop them, and no repair gang will come out until we have. And then there's the settlers. There'll be women and children with those wagons. We can't just abandon them to a gang of killers.'

'Well, you'll have to damn well do it without me,' Shadrach emphatically replied. 'I didn't sign on for no suicide mission!' So saying, he urged his weary mount to one side of the two men, his intention plain. But as he did so, there was the distinctive double click of a revolver being cocked.

'I ain't no back shooter,' Kirby quietly remarked, hefting his massive Colt. 'But if you try hightailing it, I'll put a ball right between your shoulder blades!' As he spoke, his eyes were like chips of ice, set in a face totally devoid of any comfort.

Shadrach visibly paled, and promptly reined in his animal. 'You got no call to treat me like this, after what I've been through,' he whined.

The cold-eyed Texan was unmoved. 'You ain't seen nothing yet, mister!'

'We can't let them get away with all this,' Faith Harper whispered, as she observed the Confederate raiders go about their work. Under Seward's watchful eye, his men had lopped down another stretch of telegraph poles and were dragging them to a huge bonfire close to the circled wagons. The bodies of the six men slain earlier were stacked nearby like a cord of timber. The intention was plain. Once it was time to move off, the cadavers would be tossed into the flames. Their horses and weapons had already become the spoils of war.

Jacob Smith regarded her regretfully. 'There really ain't anything I can do about it, Missus Harper. And believe me, if there was, I'd do it!'

The woman gazed up at him intently. 'After what you did for me, I believe you, Jacob. I really do. And my name is Faith. In case you hadn't noticed, I'm not married anymore.' She saw the confusion on his handsome features, and smiled regretfully. 'I'm sorry. That wasn't aimed at you. I'm just angry, that's all. Angry that this trash can do all this and get away with it.' Then, completely unexpectedly, she favoured him with a beaming smile that lit up her face.

For a moment the wagon captain was mesmerized by her beauty. Yet almost immediately, as though by divine timing, an idea came to him. 'I think there might be something could be done, but it'll have to involve someone else. You need to keep your head down for a while.' Glancing over at the Buckley wagon, he saw Jared's big frame, and his mind was suddenly made up. 'Stay here, please. I've got something needs doing.' With that, he casually drifted away.

Jared Buckley listened to his proposal with mixed emotions. Part of him was scared witless at the prospect, but then he also relished the thought of resisting the damned marauders. The big man was still feeling guilty at leaving Faith Harper to her fate, and Smith's presence before him only accentuated that emotion. He glanced at his scowling wife, and abruptly his mind was made up.

'God help me, I'll do it. You'll have to shield me, mind, and keep watch, whilst I loosen a few bolts.'

Smith nodded conspiratorially. 'Oh, I reckon I can do that.' He could have said a whole lot more, but didn't. He decided that the other man didn't yet need to know that they might both soon have blood on their hands!

Captain Seward watched with satisfaction as the final pole was heaved on to the fire. It had been a good morning's work, and there was far more to come. Using the settlers as cover, he intended to wreak havoc on the Western Union Telegraph Company. 'Toss those bodies on, and then leave it to burn, sergeant,' he ordered, before turning towards the wagons. He soon spotted the individual that he wanted, and spurred his horse over to the circled vehicles. Those men he had left on guard straightened up some at his approach.

'Time to move these wagons out, Smith.'

That man glanced up at him. 'Where to, *Captain?*'

'Just head west until I say otherwise,' came the sharp retort, and to the Confederate's mild surprise that was exactly what happened, without any argument or delay.

The wagons were strung out to their fullest extent, with the fire and devastation well behind them, when the wholly expected problem occurred: with a resounding crash, the lead wagon abruptly toppled to the left. Its driver jumped clear, landing unhurt in the grass. His wife had conveniently been walking on the far side. Predictably, the whole column came to a halt, bringing both Smith and Seward to the fore at speed.

'How the hell did this happen?' the officer demanded suspiciously. 'You must have seen it coming!'

Jared Buckley got to his feet, and glumly inspected the damage. The front of the wagon lay on its axle. The wheel had born the brunt of the collapse, with two of its oak spokes broken. Without looking at the captain, he replied, 'I've been nursing it for a while. That last rut was just too much for it.'

'So change it, and get moving,' Seward barked, not entirely convinced by the story.

Buckley sighed and glanced at Smith before responding. 'We none of us carry spares. They're too heavy and take up too much room. And since there ain't exactly any elm trees out here, I can't just fashion another.'

Seward stared at him fixedly for a moment and then

suddenly drew his huge revolver. 'Don't smart mouth me, you Yankee bastard!' he snarled. 'Or I'll blow a toe off. This shit must happen to you sodbusters plenty. How do you fix it?'

Buckley raised his hands submissively. 'Easy, mister. Easy. I can fashion a couple of new spokes. It'll just take some time, is all. I'll have to rejoin the train when I've finished.'

The other man shook his head emphatically. 'You pathetic cockchafer. You must think I came down with yesterday's rain. *Nobody* stays behind. You and your woman will have to leave the wagon and ride with someone else. You've got two minutes to shift your possibles.'

'But what about our animals?' wailed Buckley's wife.

A malicious grin crept across Seward's features. 'Happen we'll most likely eat them. Unless they're a bit stringy, like you.'

The blood drained out of Buckley's face, as he turned wide-eyed to Jacob Smith for support. But unbeknown to the settler, Smith had anticipated just such a situation, and he finally took the opportunity to speak. 'There's a number of reasons why Mister Buckley and his wagon are at the front,' he announced in deadly earnest. 'He handles a team better than any man I know, and he's also the only one I'd trust to ford a river in flood. But more importantly than that, since you killed our guide, he's the only man who knows the way!'

As he absorbed all that, Seward's jaw dropped in an unintentionally comic fashion. Then control returned, and he clamped it shut. For a long moment he stared at the damaged wheel, a faraway look in his eyes. At last he came to a decision, and one that was far from ideal. 'All right, OK. You need him that bad, *you* can help him fix his God-damn wagon. But three of my men stay with you . . . *and* I keep the scrawny bitch with me – kind of like a hostage. You give my men any trouble, an' I'll pop a cap on her. Savvy?'

Buckley's wife, who went by the name of Rebecca, stared at the Confederate officer in wide-eyed shock, then tears began to well up. She swiftly wiped them away. To Jacob Smith, it wasn't immediately apparent whether that was due to the undoubted insults, or to the very real threat; either way, Seward was unmoved by her predicament. Angrily waving the other wagons back into motion, he snarled at her, 'Go find a family that'll take you. And you'd better hope this man of yours really wants to see you again.'

Buckley smiled at her encouragingly, as he watched her walk reluctantly away. But by the time his glance fell on the wagon captain, all trace of good humour had disappeared. He well knew that his wife wasn't much to look at, but she was all he had in the world. If anything bad befell her because of Smith's little scheme, then God help him, wagon captain or no!

Taylor Shard had watched patiently as the long column moved on across the grassland until it was out of sight. Now he viewed the lone wagon through his battered spyglass with great attention. Smith and Buckley laboured around the front axle, whilst three

115

bored marauders looked on from a short distance away. Yet, although disinterested, they all had sense enough to have their weapons at the ready. All three had witnessed Smith's defence of the Harper woman's honour, and didn't intend to give him any openings.

'What are you up to, Jacob?' Shard muttered to himself, although in truth, he had a pretty fair idea. Whether completely by chance or not, the wagon captain had managed to detach himself from the main body, and now very probably had certain mayhem in mind. Thing was, up against three armed men, he and his companion could be a mite outmatched. Which was why the missing, presumed dead scout intended to even things up some. Yet unfortunately he would have to get a great deal closer, because any shooting would surely bring the rest of the gang down on them. He would need to work his way around them, approaching from their blind side. All he could fervently hope for was that Smith didn't start anything before he could get into position.

Leaving his horse ground-tethered in a small depression, the former mountain man moved swiftly, despite having to maintain an uncomfortable crouch that caused his head to start pounding again. His Spencer was cocked and ready, but he prayed that he wouldn't need to use it. Then the sound of hammering came from the wagon, which was a good sign: it meant that a genuine repair was being carried out, and also that no one had yet spotted him.

Finally he was out of the sight line of any of the five men. All he could see was the heavy, rainproof canvas above the wagon bed. It was time to close in. Transferring the carbine to his left hand, Shard drew his hunting knife, and nodded grimly with anticipation. A lot of white men had a fear of cold steel, but having spent years in the wild, he had no such qualms. His only concern was that he might not get there in time to use it!

Jacob Smith was sweating like some plantation slave down in the Deep South, and it had little to do with the physical exertion of repairing the wheel. Apart from the very real danger involved in taking on their three guards, he was also dreadfully aware of Buckley's predicament relating to his wife. And that in itself cast doubt in his mind. What if the big settler chose not to assist him, and a solo attempt then cost him his own life? Was there even any point in attempting it?

'If you boys don't get a move on, the war'll be over, an' we won't even get to see old Abe Lincoln eat humble pie,' drawled one of the guards with a snigger. In truth, the man wasn't in that much of a hurry to get back under Seward's watchful eye, but the two Yankees seemed to be taking a damn long time over their task.

Jared Buckley was in no mood for any of their taunts. His head felt like it was on fire, as he desperately tried to decide what to do. He was only too aware of Smith's meaningful glances, as that man hefted a hammer in his right hand. 'These new spokes have to be just right,' he retorted angrily, as he tapped the second one into place. 'And besides, we'll need your help to raise the wagon, if we're to get that wheel back on.'

117

'We ain't here to act as your lackeys,' a second Confederate complained.

'So go and explain to your captain why we're still back here and you ain't,'

Smith snarled. He knew that his opportunity would come when all five of them were clustered around the front axle – but the question was, did he want to take it?

As the three southerners digested their required part in raising the wagon, Buckley glanced obliquely at his companion. 'I reckon we're ready, Jacob.' And then to his captors, he added more loudly, 'Time for a bit of lifting, boys.'

The three guards regarded the large wagon without enthusiasm, but nevertheless drifted over. 'Don't you even think about trying anything,' one of them remarked. 'Any little thing happens to us, an' your wife's buzzard bait.'

'Do you think I don't know that?' Buckley murmured darkly. Then he momentarily fixed his gaze on Smith, as he continued. 'You ain't got *nothing* to fear from us, mister!'

Oblivious to the tension between the two men, the Confederates holstered their side arms and put their backs to the wagon. With Buckley alone holding the repaired wheel, Smith joined them and dropped the hammer to the ground at his feet ... within easy reach.

'Take the strain on the count of three,' the settler commanded. 'One, two, three.'

The four men heaved with all their might, and to

the accompaniment of a great deal of creaking, the axle slowly rose up from the turf. It was a heavy vehicle, and the effort required was immense. Sweat began to pour from the straining individuals, but finally it reached the required height. Buckley deftly slipped the wheel back on, and suddenly the great weight no longer existed.

In the glow of shared effort and success, their enmity was apparently forgotten, at least momentarily. Smith grinned broadly at the other three – and dropped into a crouch.

'Jacob!' Buckley roared, understanding and anger coinciding. Yet what happened next, none of them could have anticipated, because the totally unexpected attack came from behind and below: honed steel neatly severed a Confederate's Achilles' tendon, then drove, point first, down into the next one's leather boot and on through the enclosed foot.

The two victims erupted with competing screams, and fell away from the wagon in a world of hurt. Jacob Smith's first thought was that they had all been 'jumped' by a band of Sioux, and he twisted around on his haunches in horror. Then, underneath the wagon, he caught sight of Taylor Shard's manically grinning face, and all became clear. Grabbing the hammer, Smith leapt up and swung it at the third Confederate. That man had his revolver half out of its holster, but that was as far as he got: the solid flat surface of the hammer smashed into the side of his unprotected skull, instantly ending any resistance before it could begin.

119

The scout, having returned from the dead, came out from under the wagon with vengeance in his heart. The man whose foot he had skewered was completely traumatized, so he made straight for his equally unfortunate companion. Pouncing on the squirming body, Shard gleefully seized a handful of lank hair and yanked the man's head back. His already bloodstained blade sliced cleanly through the exposed throat, bringing almost instantaneous death.

With blood and grey matter seeping from the head of his own victim, Smith realized that the man was either dead or dying, and so glanced over at the sole survivor. Shard was already closing in on him, apparently intent on a clean sweep.

Although in agony from his butchered foot, the Confederate raider was still able to recognize the lethal threat. 'Please, mister,' he pleaded, keeping his hands well clear of any weapon. 'I ain't done nothing to you.'

'Well, you should have!' Shard snarled, completely unmoved. He fully intended washing his blade in even more blood. The man's survival came from a wholly unexpected source.

'Stand off, Taylor!' Smith yelled. 'We might just need a prisoner.'

The familiar voice somehow penetrated Shard's bloodlust, and very reluctantly he lowered his knife. 'You don't know how lucky you are, boy,' he murmured to the ashen-faced individual. Then he glanced over at the wagon captain, and favoured him with a lop-sided smile. 'Kind of took you all by surprise, didn't I?'

But the response to his remark wasn't anything that he could have anticipated, because before Smith could reply, Jared Buckley bellowed out, 'You stupid, bloodthirsty bastards! What's going to happen to my Rebecca now? You've as good as killed her!'

CHAPTER ELEVEN

The Confederate officer glanced behind him at the empty terrain and frowned. 'I'm beginning to think that man of yours wants rid of you,' he remarked coldly to an abruptly fraught-looking Rebecca Buckley.

It had been a day of surprises for that bigoted woman: some bad, but others not so. Having temporarily lost her husband, she had found friendship from a totally unexpected quarter. Faith Harper, whom she had always considered to be a floozy and too attractive by far, had amazingly invited her to ride on her wagon. 'Don't go fretting,' the young widow had offered consolingly. 'He'll be back presently. You'll see.' Unfortunately, Jared had so far failed to live up to that optimistic prophecy, and his continued absence was both puzzling *and* frightening.

Startled by the captain's ominous comment, Rebecca attempted a winsome smile, which, on account of her unpleasantly shrewish features, entirely failed in its aim. 'Oh, he'll turn up, captain,' she responded with forced good cheer. 'He's very reliable, is my Jared. So don't you concern yourself. Besides, you really wouldn't want to kill me, would you?'

Seward's mouth curled into a thoroughly unpleasant sneer. 'Can't think of anything *else* I'd want to do with you,' he dismissively replied, his attention suddenly taken by one of his men galloping over from the front of the wagon train.

'We got company off to the south, cap'n,' the garishly dressed enlisted man announced, as he pointed to a sizable group of horsemen in the distance. 'And this time they're kitted out like me.'

'That's all we need. Savages out for a fight!' Seward remarked disgustedly, as both his sergeant and Teague joined him.

'We're a big party. Happen they're just looking us over,' the sharpshooter opined. 'I come up against Comanches before now. If these dirt worshippers are anything like them, often times they're more interested in getting tribute than scrapping.'

'Oh, I know more than you might think about Comanches,' Seward retorted, as he pondered the situation. Thinking aloud, he added, 'Their greatness is measured by the size of their pony herd, and we do just happen to have some spare horses. If that's all these God-damned heathens are interested in, we might be able to cut a deal.' He glanced around at some of his bizarrely dressed men. 'Then again, it might give them pause when they catch sight of some of this lot.' With that he fell silent and watched as the Indians drew closer.

*

The sun-bronzed warriors of the large Sioux war party regarded the long column of wagons avariciously. Their chief had no intention of making a full-on assault against such a large company of 'white eyes': all he wanted was their just reward, in return for safe passage through the tribal lands. And yet, some of the younger braves had more on their minds than just horseflesh. They knew that the settlers travelling through their domain always brought women with them, and that they wouldn't all be pale and stringy. It might be worth having their leader's demands rebuffed, if that resulted in some authorized hit-and-run raids. After a recent, unproductive foray against their traditional enemies, the Pawnees, a little rape and pillage would address their frustrations.

Although well aware of the unspoken passions raging within his band, the Oglala chief intended to attempt peaceful contact first. Previous conflicts had taught him that the white man was best treated with caution. For some reason they had no concept of limited warfare, and if attacked would always seek bloody revenge, either by summoning the bluecoats or by banding together with other settlers. Nodding to two of the older warriors, they slowly advanced together towards the now stationary wagon train. The fact that he and his companions had left the main force behind indicated that they wished to parley.

It was only as they got nearer that the three Indians noticed that some of the interlopers scattered around

124

the wagons wore animal skins and face paint. Surprised and confused, they reined in to take stock. Were some of the white men emulating the natives as a form of flattery, or were they members of a distant tribe who had formed an alliance with the intruders? The two warriors looked to their war chief for guidance, but that man was nonplussed – and he would soon have far more to think about.

The three individuals lay on their bellies in the long grass on a small rise, some two hundred yards from the immobile wagon train. Their animals were securely tethered some distance away, so they would be neither seen nor heard. Two of the men were considering what action to take, whilst the third was pondering how best to flee without getting shot in the back.

Ransom Thatcher stared apprehensively at the Sioux war party, before quietly consulting his partner. 'You got any ideas how to handle this situation? Because as far as I can see, the odds against us just keep increasing.'

The other man grunted. 'Huh, bad odds never bothered the Texas Ranger service. Jack Hays used to take on any number of Comanches, and *win*. But as it happens, I do have a notion that should work like a charm. It means putting the settlers in harm's way. . . but then they already are. In fact, right now there's probably plenty of them wishing they'd stayed back east!'

'Hot dang! I can't wait to hear this big idea,'

Shadrach muttered sourly, but then hurriedly looked down as he caught the menace in Kirby's eye. That man frowned darkly before addressing Thatcher.

'You reckon you can bring down one of them Indian ponies with that fancy repeater of yours?'

The younger man stared at him in horror, before finally nodding his assent. 'Why would I want to do that, and what will you be doing?'

Kirby smiled knowingly. 'Oh, I'll be blowing a hole in one of those Confederate sons of bitches. Only thing is, we've got to do our killing at exactly the same time, so that both sides think they've been hit by the other. Savvy?'

Thatcher eyes widened as he realized the implications. 'Holy shit! You mean to trigger a full battle between the two sides! But what about the settlers in all of this?'

'That's the next stage. It'll be up to us to try and protect them as best we can.'

The Western Union employee was dubious. 'It's a hell of a gamble!'

'Ain't that the truth?' Kirby muttered. 'But then isn't everything? So let's just get to it.' So saying, he raised the rear ladder sight on his Sharps, and adjusted it to the estimated distance.

Thatcher watched him intently for a moment, as a related thought came to him. 'And what happens if that ranger friend of yours comes under your gun again?'

Kirby showed no hesitation. 'Then if necessary I'll kill him where he stands. But it'll serve no purpose for me to do it now, because for the sake of the settlers we need him to keep control of his men if this all goes badly.'

Despite his natural scepticism, the younger man was impressed by Kirby's logic, and so tacitly accepted the precarious plan. His next action demonstrated his consent. Keeping low, he leaned to one side and worked the Henry's lever action. Then he shifted around so that his body was almost at right angles to Kirby. 'Tell me when you're ready,' Kirby remarked. 'Then we'll fire on my count of three. And remember windage and elevation.'

'I believe I already know that,' Thatcher retorted tartly, but nevertheless gained a certain comfort from the presence of someone so obviously experienced. He tucked the rifle butt tightly into his shoulder, and drew a bead on the centre pony of the advance party. Its rider appeared to be the chief, and at such range it made sense for him to aim for the larger target of the animal, because it was critically important to actually hit something. After taking a long, deep breath to steady himself, he muttered, 'Ready.'

The Texan's voice was calm and measured. 'One . . . two . . .'

'I guess they're expecting a parley,' Seward remarked resignedly. 'Sergeant, you come with me. They might see your chevrons as a sign of prestige.' And then, in a louder voice. 'Teague, anyone out there tries anything, drop him. The rest of you, make ready. I don't trust any of those heathen sons of bitches.'

127

Turning back to the non-com, the captain gestured for him to move out and was rewarded by that man coughing up a mouthful of blood into his face. At the same time, two almost indivisible gunshots rang out, and one of the settlers cried out, 'Oh, my God!'

Desperately pawing the sticky liquid from his eyes, Seward was just in time to see the sergeant topple backwards off his horse. More blood pumped from a hole in his chest and he was obviously quite dead. Before the startled officer could react, a collective howl of dismay and anger rose up from the Sioux war party. Their chief had just been pitched forwards over the head of his dying pony and lay in the grass, temporarily stunned and unable to speak.

Seward switched his angry gaze to his sharpshooter, but that man reacted with a genuinely forceful rebuttal. 'No way was that me, cap'n. In fact it weren't anyone here. And there were two shots came from out yonder. I reckon someone's setting us up!'

The two flanking warriors peered down at their winded leader with a mixture of shock and outrage. Unlike the white men, their heated emotions didn't allow for any considered deliberations relating to the origins of the gunshot. It only mattered that they were under attack, and *nobody* struck with impunity at the Sioux! As one of them slid off his pony to attend to the gasping chief, the other turned to the infuriated war party and bellowed out, '*Hoka Hey*!'

The assembled warriors needed no further urging. '*Hoka Hey*!' came the eager response, and digging

128

their heels in, they surged forwards, yelling out foul taunts and madly waving their weapons. They swept past the struggling chief at breakneck speed, and on towards the column of wagons. As that infuriated individual sucked air into his lungs, he regained the power of speech.

'Call them back at once,' he breathlessly commanded. 'One dead pony is not worth the lives of my warriors.' Yet even as he spoke, he knew that it was too late, because any chance of them hearing was abruptly drowned out by a ragged fusillade.

'Oh shit! This is all we need,' Teague muttered, but any further observation was lost as the uneven volley crashed out on Seward's command. The Confederate irregulars, now reduced to just less than thirty, were armed with a mishmash of weapons, from British Enfield rifled muskets to sawn-off shotguns – but all of them knew how to shoot . . . *and* they didn't scare easy!

A serious amount of lead flew at the fast approaching warriors, and much of it struck home. As a cloud of sulphurous smoke drifted off on the unusually light prairie breeze, screams of pain mingled with the beating hoofs. With a number of Indians either dead or wounded, the charge momentarily slowed. Yet the Sioux were natural cavalry, and even without their fallen leader their blood was up. With cries of defiance, they came on again with renewed vigour.

'Get back behind the wagons!' Seward bellowed at his men. He knew that in line, the wagons were vulnerable, but the time for circling them had long gone.

By coincidence, he soon found himself using the Harper wagon as cover, and was startled when a female voice shouted in his ear.

'You have to arm the settlers,' Faith cried out earnestly.

The captain wasn't having any of that. 'Like hell I do! Any sodbuster makes a move for the weapons, he'll end up dead as a wagon tyre.' Dismissing her and the settlers from his mind, he drew a bead on the nearest Indian and fired.

The sound of sustained shooting in the distance did nothing for Jared Buckley's fragile mental state. 'Oh, my God!' he cried. 'Rebecca's in danger. We've got to hurry!'

The three men were sat abreast on the bench seat of his wagon, as it moved steadily west. The two dead guards had been left to rot, because as the scout had said, 'Even buzzards have got to eat!' The wounded survivor had been dumped in the back, a scavenged shirt tied around his badly mutilated foot. His wrists were bound, and any fight had gone out of him. All he seemed capable of was fitful moaning. As was usually the case, to the victors go the spoils, and they now possessed a selection of weaponry, along with three horses trotting along behind.

Taylor Shard, having been apprised of the whole situation by Smith, would have none of Buckley's exhortations. 'Don't be a damned fool, man. If the wagon train *is* under attack, then those poxy Confederates will have more to think on than blowing holes in your wife. And if we go blundering in there full chisel trying to rescue her from who knows what, we'll just end up dead.'

'Damn right,' the wagon captain agreed. 'What we need to do is leave your wagon here, and close in on foot. Take a look-see without being spotted.'

The big settler, assailed by one torment after another, was horrified. 'I can't just leave it untended. All I've got in the world is in this.'

Shard glanced back at the sparse belongings and shrugged. 'Seems to me like you've got a bit of catching up to do, mister.' Then, as the casual – and in truth, unintentional – insult began to register with the other man, he moved on swiftly. 'Which do you value more, this little lot or your wife?'

Buckley scowled at him. 'My wife, of course.'

The scout slapped him companionably on his broad back. 'Good man. And think of it this way. You won't be leaving it all alone because our passenger will be chained to one of the wheels.'

Rebecca Buckley screamed as a howling savage, daubed in vivid ochre, raced towards her, brandishing a razor-sharp tomahawk. With absolutely nothing to defend herself, and all the Confederates otherwise occupied in the absolute mayhem around her, she realized with awful clarity that she was going to die. Then, without any warning, a heavy cooking pot flew past her and struck the warrior a glancing blow on his left shoulder.

'Get away from her, you bastard,' Faith yelled from

under the canvas cover, but it was too little, too late. Shrugging off the sharp pain, the startled aggressor glanced over at the younger woman, and all of a sudden killing was no longer uppermost in his fevered mind. Leaping at the wagon, he struck Rebecca with an almost casual blow with his left fist that nevertheless sent her reeling back on to the bench seat, and then over the far side to the hard ground.

Faith grabbed a wooden broom and swung it at her frightening assailant, but he just ducked under it and then laughed in her face as if to say, 'I'm going to enjoy this!'

As the Sioux climbed on to the seat towards her, a scream began to form in her throat. For a brief moment his eyes gleamed exultantly ... and then everything changed. As she stared in disbelief, he suddenly pitched forwards, coughing blood over her cotton dress. A large hole had appeared in his back, and whatever had penetrated him was clearly causing his life to sap away. If she hadn't been so relieved at her totally unexpected reprieve, Faith might just have wondered at the fact that there was nobody in direct line of sight behind her dying attacker!

With a grim smile of satisfaction, Kirby lowered the Sharps' breechblock and blew into the smoking chamber. That had been a neat effort, catching the Indian just before he disappeared into the wagon's interior.

'Good shot,' Thatcher acknowledged admiringly, as he watched for the next required intervention. He was only too aware that he could not equal that sort of marksmanship.

The scene unfolding before them was one of pure pandemonium, with mounted Sioux sweeping through the gaps between the immobile wagons, shooting and hacking at anyone in their path. It included the bizarre sight of white men dressed as Indians fighting genuine natives. And yet, despite their apparent superiority in numbers, the Oglala warriors were not having it all their own way. They had expected to be taking on a group of untrained settlers, not disciplined soldiery, and many of the ponies galloping around no longer possessed riders.

'Remember,' Kirby remarked. 'Only shoot if a settler's threatened. With any luck, Seward's boys will be getting thinned out some.'

The other man merely grunted. He didn't need telling twice. And besides, he suddenly had a genuine target. One of the painted warriors astride his pony was hacking away at a canvas awning like a berserker. Knowing that he would struggle to hit the moving Indian, Thatcher again aimed at the animal. Even as the butt recoiled into his shoulder, he knew he'd got it right.

The pony slewed sideways, taking its rider with it – but with a fine display of athleticism, he rolled once and leapt to his feet. For a brief moment he was upright and motionless and Thatcher, having rapidly worked the lever action, was ready. The Henry crashed out again, its bullet penetrating the warrior's lower back and sending him down to join his stricken pony.

Kirby was genuinely impressed. 'You're getting to be quite the marksman. If you ever get tired of working for Western Union, look me up.'

And then, quite suddenly, it was all over. . . for the present. The surviving Oglala raced away from the wagons, leaving their dead and wounded behind them. But they only retreated to extreme rifle range, where they joined their recovered and very angry leader. Their continued presence was guaranteed to aggravate the Confederate captain.

'God damn it all to hell!' Seward angrily exclaimed. His full beard was stained with his sergeant's blood, and his extreme exasperation was plain for all to see. 'We just don't need all this shit! Indian fighting isn't what we came up here for!' Suddenly aware that all eyes were on him, he drew in several deep breaths and quickly regained control. There was much to be done, and it was up to him to provide the necessary leadership.

'Reload all your weapons immediately and then see to the wounded,' he barked out. 'Help ours where you can, and kill theirs. You settlers, get these wagons circled. Pronto. It's your lives as much as ours, and those cockchafers might not be finished with us yet.'

His clear orders soon brought some stability out of the chaos. The sound of intermittent gunshots brought grim satisfaction to some, as the enemy wounded were put to death. And yet, even as the wagon circle closed around them, Teague reminded his commander of another serious difficulty.

'Whatever else those dirt worshippers have got in mind, we've got a bigger problem. Whoever started all this is still out there, and they sure as hell ain't on our side. I was watching. They kilt at least two of them vermin, but only when they threatened the settlers.'

'Where away?' Seward demanded.

'In the long grass, about two hundred yards that'a way,' the sharpshooter replied, pointing to the west. 'And they sure know what they're about.'

Seward scanned the horizon and sighed, but the enlisted man hadn't finished with him quite yet. 'One of them is using a Sharps, just like whoever jumped us back at the Pony Express station.' He favoured the officer with a telling glance, whilst stubbornly continuing to avoid any display of deference. 'Kind of makes you think, don't it?'

CHAPTER TWELVE

'Where the hell's Shadrach got to?' Kirby hissed angrily.

Startled, Ransom Thatcher twisted around on the grass and spotted the so-called hired gun in the distance, running for his life. Angrily, he brought the Henry to his shoulder. He had never before shot a man in the back, but that was about to change. And yet, just as he drew a fine bead, his companion pulled down on the barrel.

'Better not,' the Texan remarked. 'The fighting's ended over there. Any more shooting here will give away our position.' It was good advice, but unfortunately Shadrach's hurried departure had already been noticed, and all hell was about to descend upon him. None of which would have mattered, but for the fact that he was making for three tethered horses!

The Sioux chief was mounted again, and the additional height enabled him to see the lone individual fleeing westward. Rapidly concluding that it had to be a fugitive from the wagon train, he barked out an order and was soon at the head of six warriors as they raced in pursuit. As they rode, their leader made it very plain that the kill should be his.

Shadrach's confidence grew as he neared the horses. But unused to running, he was sorely winded, and the effort involved in maintaining the pace meant that he hadn't noticed the cessation of hostilities behind him. So it was all the more shocking when he heard the pounding of unshod hoofs. Glancing back, he saw the seven Oglala closing in, and any strength remaining in his trembling legs immediately vanished.

'Oh Jesus,' he moaned, because there really wasn't anything else to say. Their speed was such that he realized he had no chance of reaching the horses. He also recognized that any resistance would be futile, though a little corner of his mind drove him to an attempt anyway. Drawing and cocking his revolver, Shadrach drew a shaky bead on the leading horseman.

The chief saw the threat, and with consummate ease urged his pony to one side. The whole group abruptly split in two, so they came charging down on either flank of their terrified victim. Suddenly unsure who to tackle first, his nerve left him and he simply froze with fear.

As planned, the chief reached him first. There would be no counting coup: too many of his warriors had died, and all he desired was revenge. Lowering his war lance, he expertly drove the razor-sharp point into the pathetic white man's stomach. Having literally skewered his prey, the Sioux disdainfully released his hold on the lance and carried on towards the three saddled horses that were his prize. He knew full well that the fugitive was finished, and so it proved.

Shadrach, overwhelmed by the shocking pain, didn't even cry out. He just toppled over on to the grass and lay in a foetal position, completely helpless as his lifeblood drained away. His Indian killer, buoyed up by the easy personal victory and unexpected loot, whooped with triumph – though he wasn't so excited that he didn't recognize the possibilities: three saddled horses meant three riders, and yet they had only found one.

Issuing a series of orders, he soon had one warrior returning to the main party, leading the spoils of war. The rest of them spread out and began a steady sweep to the east. The chief briefly stopped to retrieve his bloodied lance. As he bent over the dying white man, his obsidian eyes registered nothing, but in his heart there was a surge of joy as he heaved out the vicious weapon. Its withdrawal was accompanied by a very satisfying sucking sound. Revelling in his repossession of the gory item, he leapt astride his pony and rejoined the others in their search.

'Oh shit, that's torn it,' the Texan exclaimed, struck by the unpleasant realization that they would now have to remain on foot. 'Looks like we're well and truly between a rock and a hard place!' Having witnessed Shadrach's gruesome fate, he had no illusions about what was coming their way. 'That silly bastard's given us away, *and* got himself kilt into the bargain.'

Ransom Thatcher viewed the six advancing natives with calculated resolution. Patting the stock of his Henry, he announced, 'This fine gun can handle 'em all, and then some. You keep watch over the wagons, while I see to business.' So saying, he twisted around until he faced west, and then rose up from the grass to 'take a knee'. With adrenalin pumping through his body, it never occurred to him that he was effectively placing his life in Kirby's hands – but even if it had, he would still have acted in the same way. Levelling his rifle, the young man took aim at the nearest warrior.

'Teague, drop that son of a bitch,' Seward instinctively commanded, as he watched the figure suddenly rise up from the grass. The fact that the man was facing in the opposite direction counted for nothing. Then, recalling the shots that triggered the Sioux attack, he added, 'I don't know who the hell he is, but I sure do reckon he means us harm. It's just plumb dandy that those heathen sons of bitches have flushed him for us.'

The sharpshooter nodded enthusiastically. After all, killing was what he did best. 'Be my pleasure, cap'n!' he replied, which was about as close as he ever got to demonstrating any respect for rank. 'But someone needs to cover me, 'cause just like snakes there's more than one of them in that long grass.'

Moving over to the wagon directly opposite his quarry's position, the southerner retracted the hammer of his cherished Whitworth rifle and took careful aim at the unprotected broad back, using the

139

vehicle's side for support. At a mere two hundred yards, and with his uncanny skill, it was a sure shot. Such was his supreme self-confidence that he didn't even bother to raise the rear ladder sight. Another enlisted man, known for his ability with a long gun, arrived at his side and levelled an Enfield rifle.

'Anybody else moves over there, blast him,' Teague ordered. So far, all that either of them could see was the individual facing the Sioux. And it was only as that man opened *repeating* fire on the Indians that a hint of doubt entered the sharpshooter's mind, because that sure as hell wasn't a Sharps in action.

The heavy calibre lead ball struck Teague in the centre of his face, utterly destroying his squat nose, and exiting the back of his head in a deluge of brain tissue and blood. Death was instantaneous, and he collapsed to the ground, his highly prized weapon still unfired. The man with the Enfield dutifully fired at the smoke, but of course his target had already moved.

Ransom Thatcher squeezed the trigger and then just kept on firing. For a world mostly used only to single-shot rifles, it was an awesome display of modern firepower. Bullet after bullet flew at the advancing Sioux, knocking them down like ninepins. Unable to get to close quarters, not one of them was given a chance to fight back, and so their numerical superiority counted for nothing. Thatcher was aided by an increasingly strong breeze, which blew away the powder smoke, leaving his aim unaffected. It was as though he possessed a charmed life, because in the heat of the moment, the young man was dimly aware of a single crash behind him, and yet discounted it immediately. After all, didn't he have a former Texas Ranger watching his back?

As yet another pony fell under him, it was the chief who died first, his neck broken in the fall. Then a gut-shot warrior swayed sideways, swiftly losing the battle to stay mounted. As a third Indian in seemingly as many seconds was struck a mortal blow, the rest abruptly recognized that they were up against a terri-fying new weapon – and with the death of their leader, their 'medicine' had irreversibly gone bad. Ignoring the valuable riderless ponies, they veered away and desperately tried to put some distance between them-selves and their lethal foe.

Working the lever action like a madman, Thatcher continued to fire at the retreating warriors, and brought at least one more of them crashing to the ground. It wasn't just that he had an insatiable desire for blood, he was also mature enough to realize that the more damage he could inflict, the less likely they were to continue the fight.

Seward gazed in horror as his sharpshooter's skull appeared to explode like a ripe melon. Their losses were mounting, and this was by far their most serious fatality. Glancing around at his remaining men, he could see that the shock of it had affected them all. Teague had been far from popular, but his deadly pro-ficiency had never been in doubt. Under mounting pressure, it took a concentrated effort of will for the captain to organize his thoughts.

'You men at the front,' he shouted. 'Lay down some fire on whoever's over there!' But of course by then the Indian killer had expended his magazine and dropped back down out of sight. 'The rest of you, keep an eye on those God-damn savages.'

As gunshots rattled out, Seward detailed two men to remove Teague's body from sight. Of all the casualties, his would have the strongest detrimental effect on his men's morale. Then, satisfied that he had done all he could, the officer moved forward to join those firing at their mysterious attackers. Had it occurred to him, he would have done well to check on the settlers!

Shard, Buckley and Smith had advanced from the east completely unnoticed. They had waited for the wagons to be circled, and the shooting to start again before making the final dash. There were plenty of blood-soaked cadavers scattered around, and the wailing of wounded in one of the wagons, but no sign of any Confederate guards. The various conflicts were obviously taking their toll.

Suddenly spotting his wife peering anxiously from one of the wagons, Jared Buckley made straight for it. Climbing in through the 'puckering strings' at the back of her temporary home, he moved lightly for such a big man. Knowing that Rebecca might well cry out, he closed in from behind and wrapped a horny hand over her face. Panic-stricken, for a brief moment she struggled helplessly until he whispered in her ear, 'Shhh, my dear. It's only me.' Then, after pulling her

142

back under canvas away from prying eyes, he released his grip.

Twisting around, Rebecca stared at him wide-eyed for what seemed like an age, before suddenly exclaiming, 'You big oaf! You scared me half to death!' Then she hugged him long and hard, displaying a depth of emotion that surprised him by its intensity.

The wagon suddenly swayed as Faith Harper climbed aboard, and sadly the pleasantly unexpected intimacy was over, because that woman had a crucial question. 'I'm glad to see you back safe, Jared, but what happened to the guards that went with you?'

Buckley's explanation came in a rush. 'Two paroled to Jesus, one chained to our wagon back yonder. And Mister Shard ain't dead. He and Jacob did the killing. They're waiting in the grass nearby.'

Faith nodded calmly, as though she had expected such news. 'Could be we'll all have blood on our hands soon, because this is the best chance we're gonna get to chase off those varmints. They're occupied shooting at some strangers off to the west, and there's no one guarding the wagon with all your guns.'

The big man sighed as he realized the implications of that statement. He had no appetite for brutal violence, but it appeared as though there was no choice. Nodding reluctantly, he gently patted Rebecca and then clambered out of the back of the wagon to rejoin his fellow conspirators.

A volley of lead scythed through the long grass above

Thatcher and the Texan. Although at a similar elevation to the wagons, the two men were protected by a
slight undulation in the ground that acted somewhat
like a glacis around a fortress. Nevertheless, they were
in a thoroughly unpleasant situation.

Thatcher was doing his best to reload the Henry,
but the necessity to remain flat made that task very dif-
ficult. With the weapon lying at a right angle to his
body, and the muzzle facing him, he had released the
tab at the end of the long cylindrical magazine and
was laboriously slotting fresh cartridges into it.

'I tell you, this is one hell of a good firearm,' he
shouted over the din. 'But if I ever meet Benjamin
Tyler Henry, I'll be sure to give him some tips. This
thing's crying out for a loading gate in the side, and
maybe a nice wooden forestock.'

'I'd be happy just to be able to get a shot off,' the
Texan retorted. '*I tell you*, if those Indians pull out,
we'll be in deep shit. Their presence is the only reason
Seward doesn't have his men rush us!'

The surviving members of the Sioux war party stared
in amazement at the conflict that had erupted
between the opposing white men. Whilst it was deeply
puzzling, it also seemed to imply that *they* were no
longer considered to be a threat, which, although
rather insulting, wasn't actually far from the truth.
The loss of their chief, along with many warriors, and
the fact that the wagons were now defensively circled,
all indicated that it was time to withdraw. At least they
had captured three horses, with saddles and various

144

accoutrements to show for the encounter, and these would have to suffice. It was time to go. '*Hoka Hey*!'

'Those damned savages are pulling out, captain,' an enlisted man yelled, and suddenly the Confederate officer had another string to his bow.

Swivelling on his heels, Seward watched as the Sioux moved off to the southwest. He decided that their departure was unlikely to be a ruse, as the heathens had lost a lot of men, and there had to be softer targets somewhere else on the Northern Plains. Which meant that he could now close in on the unknown assassins. They would have to die, of course, but he was also keen to discover their identity. And then, finally, he might be able to continue his assault on the North's communications. Even though he now had fewer than twenty men fit for duty, it would be enough. Amazingly, nowhere in his scheming did he take into account the continued presence of the settlers.

'You men facing south, mount up,' he bellowed. 'The rest of you keep pouring it on. It's high time we found out who owns that Sharps!'

Shard, Buckley and Smith moved stealthily around the outer circle, until they came to the wagon containing all the confiscated weapons. Some of the settlers watched them curiously, but most of them had their eyes glued to the one-sided conflict playing out on the western edge of the circle. Amazingly, the Confederates still didn't have a single guard posted.

'Guess they must have their minds on something else,' Shard remarked with a wry smile.

Buckley climbed into the back of the wagon, and began to pass the assorted firearms out. Strangely, he moved without any great urgency, as though in a dream, but he was about to find himself under immense pressure.

'Whoever's been shooting at these God-damned wreckers is about to get rousted out,' Jacob Smith announced, as he watched some of the Confederates mount their animals. 'We're never going to get a better time to fight back.' Glancing at the scout, he queried, 'Are you up for it?'

'Damn right I am,' that man responded. Fixing his gimlet eyes on Buckley, he ordered, 'Get these guns back to your people and tell them to fight for their lives.'

Buckley had known that this moment must come, but now that it had, he was horrified. 'W-what are *you* gonna be doing?' he stammered.

Smith glared angrily at him. 'What Taylor and I have been doing since the start . . . fighting back. Now get moving, before I kick seven shades of shit out of you!' With that, he turned away and glanced keenly at Shard. Favouring him with a broad grin, he asked, 'You *really* sure you're ready for this?'

'I was born ready!'

And so the two men, one with his Spencer and holstered Colt, and the other with a brace of Colt Navy Sixes, walked steadily away from the wagon into the centre of the circle. They were deliberately displaying

146

themselves, because they wanted the settlers to see it all. And they picked their moment to perfection. Seward had just ordered his mounted men forward in two groups, one on either flank, and was exhorting his remaining irregulars to keep up a heavy fire on their mysterious assailants. There were eight of them, and they all had their backs to the deadly new threat.

Neither Taylor Shard nor Jacob Smith would normally have shot a man in the back, but this was something entirely different. Their survival depended on it. Tucking the Spencer tightly into his shoulder, Shard fired without hesitation. At his side, but a little apart, the wagon captain triggered the right-hand Colt, and two men cried out with pain and shock.

For a brief moment, neither Seward nor his men could comprehend what was happening. Shard rapidly levered in another cartridge and cocked the hammer before they could react. He took fresh aim just as his intended victim began to turn. The bullet struck the man in the shoulder, knocking him back, but not killing him. Smith had been even quicker. Even as he tilted his smoking revolver to cock it, he fired the left-hand gun. Not used to shooting with that hand, his aim was slightly off true, and the .36 calibre ball hit his victim's right arm, shattering it just above the elbow.

'The bastards are behind us!' Seward bellowed somewhat needlessly. He and his men twisted around to face their new assailants, which instantly meant they were no longer supporting their mounted comrades.

*

147

Over in the long grass, Thatcher and Kirby were in desperate straits. Immobilized by overwhelming fire, they were completely unable to offer any resistance. And then they heard the pounding of shod hoofs, as the Confederate horsemen raced for their flanks, and they knew that their time had come.

'If it counts for anything, I'm right proud to have ridden with you,' Thatcher called over.

'Likewise,' came the terse retort. 'It's just a crying shame I never got to face down that bastard, Seward.' But the words were barely out of his mouth, when suddenly they were no longer under fire. Then they were able to make out the sounds of rather more distant shooting. Whatever was happening had undoubtedly given them a new lease on life. 'Take the north side and blast the sons of bitches,' Kirby commanded jubilantly.

Thatcher needed no further urging. Rising up out of the grass, he shouldered his Henry and began to blaze away at the mounted figures. Behind him, Kirby fired his Sharps. The formidable gun blew his victim clean out of the saddle. Then, letting it fall to the ground, the former ranger drew his Colt Walker. As the two men stood back to back, the most powerful revolver in the West belched forth death, whilst all the time there came the repeated discharges of Thatcher's rifle.

It was quite simply too much for the Confederate horsemen. With their covering fire abruptly and inexplicably absent, the surviving riders viciously reined around, dug in their heels and raced for what they thought would be the safety of the wagons. Unknowingly, they were about to be reinforcements for their leader's unwanted and unexpected battle with Shard and Smith.

CHAPTER THIRTEEN

'You can't leave those two to fight alone,' Faith Harper angrily chided Buckley, as repeated gunshots crashed out. She and Rebecca had followed him to the weapons cache, and neither was prepared to stand idly by. 'They're doing it for you and everyone else in this wagon train. *Help them*!'

Jared Buckley stared hard at her, still desperately torn by the indecision that Rebecca's sour dominance had ingrained in him. Amazingly, it was his much changed wife who finally made up his mind for him. 'I was wrong before, and Faith's right now,' she remarked firmly. 'Take up one of those guns and help them. We'll pass these out to the others.' She smiled warm encouragement at him, which in itself was something new.

'What the hell!' he retorted. 'It's time we got rid of the damned rebels!' With that, he took up a shotgun and some shells and went looking for trouble. He didn't have far to go.

Between them, Shard and Smith had brought down

two more Confederates, but Seward and his men were fighting back, and the scout now had fresh blood on his buckskins. He was also about to fire the last cartridge in his Spencer. Then he saw the returning horsemen and his heart sank. 'Oh Jesus,' he yelled. 'Now we're for it!'

A shotgun crashed out just off to his right, and he flinched involuntarily. Then as blood spurted from the utterly destroyed features of one of their enemies, he realized with a start that the shooter was with him, rather than against him. Even more amazingly, from all around him there came a collective growl of anger, and more shots began to rattle out. The settlers had finally found the will to fight back, and somehow the former mountain man knew that there would be no stopping them.

With his men dying around him, Captain Seward gazed with almost uncontrolled rage at the once docile individuals emerging from their wagons. Two women that he recognized, one attractive, the other much less so, were handing out firearms to suddenly willing recipients. With the whole wagon train taking up arms against them, and two unknown professionals undoubtedly coming up at the rear, he very reluctantly took a command decision.

'Mount up and head south!' he bellowed out. Then, as if to clarify the parlous turn of events, the captain added, 'Flee for your lives. Every man for himself!'

Those already mounted needed no further persuasion. Again spurring their animals into motion, they gladly left the deadly confines of the wagon circle. Those few remaining on foot were not so lucky. With more and more men joining Shard and Smith, vast amounts of hot lead were being unleashed. The fact that Seward was able to make good his escape was in part because much of the shooting was ill judged and went wide. He also carried the luck of the devil with him, as none of his enlisted men had the same good fortune. They all went down in a welter of blood and gore, shot to pieces by the suddenly emboldened settlers.

The former Texas Ranger spotted the bearded figure of his old comrade-in-arms as that man burst clear of the wagons and raced south. The fugitive had quickly worked his fresh horse up to a dead run, and was rapidly putting distance between himself and the wagons. Shaking his head regretfully, Kirby made some rapid calculations as he adjusted the ladder sight on his Sharps. He knew full well that he couldn't allow the Confederate raider to escape a second time. It would be an awkward shot, because his target was moving fast and at a tricky angle. There was a lot to take into account, but that wouldn't be the first time.

Consciously inhaling steadily, he took careful aim at the fast moving animal with the precision long gun, and banished all other considerations from his mind. After squeezing the first of the double-set triggers, he waited a moment longer, held his breath and fired. He had been by no means certain of the shot, and so it was with a mixture of regret and exhilaration that he watched the poor creature trip and execute an almost perfect somersault, taking its rider with it.

With bated breath, Kirby strained for any sign of movement. The stricken horse twitched and shifted, but was obviously down to stay. 'Don't get up, God damn it,' he muttered softly, but then watched with great sadness as Seward slowly staggered to his feet. 'Aw, God dang!'

Ransom Thatcher observed his companion with great interest. Now he would finally discover where the older man's loyalties really lay. Which would triumph, Western Union's cash bounty, or some vague past association? He was well aware that some men are only ever motivated by greed, but he hadn't quite made up his mind about Kirby. He was suddenly aware of that man eyeing him questioningly, and he had his answer ready. Gesturing with his Henry, he responded, 'At that distance I ain't got a chance with this piece . . . or probably any other for that matter.'

The other man grunted something unintelligible, and with obvious reluctance lowered his weapon's breechblock. Slipping in another paper cartridge and closing the breech, he replaced the percussion cap and then slowly returned the Sharps to his shoulder. Staring fixedly down the barrel's length, Kirby drew a bead on his former comrade. Seward was swaying on his feet, as though the plain's relentless wind was too strong for him. Then, with obvious effort, he turned away and took an unsteady pace forward.

'You can't let him get away,' Thatcher pointedly remarked. 'Not after what he's done.'

153

'Do you think I don't know that?' Kirby snapped back, as he retracted the hammer. His prey was moving slowly and painfully. This shot would be far easier than the first. . . if he could take it. Suddenly very conscious of Thatcher's eyes on him, he could feel beads of sweat forming on his forehead. With his mouth abruptly as parched as sun-dried rawhide, he squeezed the first trigger. Drawing in a deep breath had suddenly become painful. His forefinger closed over the second trigger – and he froze.

Then a single shot rang out from behind him with startling clarity, and he saw Seward spin round and drop out of sight. Wide-eyed with surprise, Kirby himself spun round to see where it had come from.

'This is a damned fine gun,' Shard observed, as he hefted the smoking Whitworth. 'Used to have me an old Hawken just like it.'

'Did you kill him?' Smith queried.

'Nah, just winged him. But it'll have knocked the starch out of him some.'

Jacob Smith glanced around until his eyes settled on a father and his full-grown son. 'Will. You and Seth get mounted and bring that fella back,' he commanded. 'Be careful he doesn't draw on you. He's a tricky one.'

'Sure thing, Jacob,' came the eager reply. 'Be right happy to.' Now that the real danger was over, suddenly everyone was a hero.

As the two settlers left leading a spare horse, the wagon captain and his scout turned their attention to the two men walking towards them from the west.

'You ever seen them before, Taylor?'

'Nope.'

'Best keep your Spencer on them until we find out their intentions.' Smith remarked. 'Your enemy's enemy isn't *always* your friend.' Suddenly sensing someone at his elbow, he turned to find the delectable figure of Faith Harper beaming up at him.

'I just wanted to thank you for everything that you've done for us . . . and me,' she remarked loudly. Then, in a far softer and huskier tone, she added, 'You've turned out to be quite a man, Jacob Smith.'

'What about me? Ain't I done anything?' Shard asked, giving a pretty fair display of righteous indignation. In truth, he appeared far more battered and bloody than the wagon captain.

The young woman laughed brightly. 'More than we could ever repay you for, Mister Shard.'

'Huh, we'll see about that,' the scout chuckled. Then his expression darkened as he regarded the approaching men, and he slowly stepped to one side. 'That cuss with the scarred neck looks like he's seen some action in his time.'

Smith said nothing. Instead he watched and waited until the strangers reached the wagons. To his mind, they made a rather odd couple, and couldn't have just appeared out of sheer happenstance. 'That'll do fine just about there, gents,' he remarked easily, but there was no mistaking the iron in his words.

Kirby and Thatcher came to a halt, their weapons held loosely at their sides. Taking his lead from the older man, Thatcher remained silent as they waited to see what transpired.

The wagon captain regarded them steadily, and then asked what suddenly seemed like a very natural question. 'Since you're not badged up, I'm guessing you two fellas must be some kind of government men, huh?'

A broad smile crept across Thatcher's face. 'Look's like you've made us, mister, or at least got close. We work for the Western Union Telegraph Company, which *is* right popular in Washington at the moment. Leastways it will be if the damn telegraph line ever gets finished.'

'You saw our bona fides when my partner sent those savages to perdition,' the Texan added.

'Reckon you must be after the murdering fire-starters that took over our wagons,' Shard remarked, as he gradually lowered the barrel of his Spencer.

'Ain't that the truth,' replied Kirby, who hadn't missed the welcome but somewhat furtive movement. 'And one of you just bagged the leader.'

'That'd be me,' the scout answered.

'Nice shot!'

'Thank you kindly.'

There followed a short, but not uncomfortable silence, as the four of them waited for the riders to return. When they did, Kirby's jaw tightened as he observed that Seward had been flung across the saddle like a sack of potatoes. The eldest of the two settlers dismounted with a flourish, and sauntered over to his wounded prisoner. 'This scum belly don't look so tough now,' he gleefully remarked. Grabbing him by his trousers belt, he gave a sharp heave, bringing the wounded man to earth with great force.

Seward, with blood soaking his tunic jacket and eyes tightly shut, gave a great moan of pain. Kirby, his face abruptly set like granite, strode over to the settler. 'You must be a real dangerous hombre to treat an injured man like that, but here's something for you to think on. You lay another hand on him, an' I'll take this Colt Walker to your skull. Savvy?'

Suddenly ashen-faced and deflated, the settler rapidly backed off.

'OK, Will. You and your son can get about your business,' Smith quietly remarked. 'We'll handle this.' Turning to face the scarred Texan, he continued. 'It's not often I see one of those big horse pistols nowadays, and yet this Confederate son of a bitch is toting one as well.'

Ransom Thatcher noisily cleared his throat, but before he could say anything the wounded prisoner, reacting to a voice from the past, had opened his eyes and was staring up fixedly at the former ranger. '*You*!'

Kirby grimly returned the stare. 'The very same.'

Seward shook his head with disbelief, but then immediately regretted it and winced. 'And back at the swing station, with the Sharps?'

'Yeah.'

'Sweet Jesus,' the Confederate exclaimed. 'Of all the people to have hunting me, it has to be you.'

'You should have stayed in Texas,' Kirby retorted.

'So should you.'

157

For long moments the two men just stared at each other in silence, as though mutually recalling past memories. Such was the intensity of the mood that no one else interrupted. It was Seward who finally broke the reverie.

'So what will happen to me, now that you've brought me to heel?'

Thatcher had all the answers to that. 'We'll be taking you back to Omaha. Our boss, Mister Ezra Cornell, will be right pleased to see you. After what you've done, you'll be lucky if you're treated as a prisoner of war. You deserve a firing squad . . . or maybe even a lynching. But then I suppose you're at least wearing some kind of uniform, unlike a lot of your men, so you could just end up in a stockade for the duration.'

Seward cast a scornful glance at the young man, before returning his attention to his fellow Texan. 'Just who the hell's this turd, anyhu?'

Despite the situation, Kirby chuckled. 'He doesn't like you burning his telegraph poles and murdering his workmen.'

'Oh, I see.'

Jacob Smith had had enough. 'These sons of bitches have cost us plenty of wasted time, and we're burning daylight. If it were up to me, I'd just put a ball in his head. But if you have to do it all legal, then this fella needs patching up and clapping in irons. It's what he did to me. We'll help you round up some horses, but then we'll have to be on our way. We've got to cross the Rockies before the snows come.' In truth, he had far more on his mind than just traversing some massive mountain barrier. Having survived his desperate struggle against the marauders, he was now more than ever hoping that his future would include Faith Harper.

'That sounds reasonable,' Thatcher acknowledged. Then in a far harsher tone he commanded, 'Come on you cockchafer, on your feet.'

With no one prepared to assist him, it took the Confederate captain a lot of painful effort to get upright. Blood seeped from his right shoulder, where the bullet from Teague's Whitworth had struck him. Again ignoring everyone else, he fixed his gaze on his old comrade-in-arms. There was a strange intensity to his eyes that hinted at tremendous suppressed emotion.

'Could *you* survive in some poxy stockade, without even the stars for company?' he asked in hushed tones. 'For men like us, that would be worse than any death sentence.'

No one else affected any interest, but to Kirby that seemed as close to pleading as a man like Seward could get. 'Some might say you don't deserve considerations, what with all those killings an' all.'

The captain grunted. 'We've all of us done bad deeds. And if the South is to survive, there'll be plenty more yet. . . only I won't be doing them. Will I?'

The question was loaded with meaning, but only Kirby absorbed it. Thatcher was busy reloading his new-fangled repeater, whilst the overlanders were making preparations to depart. 'You know what you're asking, don't you?'

Seward favoured him with a faint smile. 'Reckon it's in your gift.' Then he turned away and just stood, swaying slightly, like a willow in the breeze.

The temporary Western Union employee knew what he had to do, and that it had nothing to do with the job that he was being paid for. But that didn't make it any the easier. Suddenly aware of the sweat coating his palms, he cocked and lifted his Sharps in one fluid movement. The muzzle lined up with the back of Seward's skull, so close that Kirby felt as though he could touch the greying hair. But again he froze, unable to take that last, irrevocable action.

Then, from very close by, Thatcher barked out, 'What the hell are you about?'

Closing his eyes, the former Texas Ranger squeezed hard on the trigger, and was rewarded by a loud crash.

He had finally got the job done!